5

THE DAYSTAR VOYAGES

REVENGE OF THE SPACE PIRATE

GILBERT MORRIS
AND DAN MEEKS

MOODY PRESS

CHICAGO

To my father, Joseph Daniel Meeks

Dad, I know that my growing up wasn't easy—for either of us! Since you passed on, I've had a lot of time to think. I'll never forget the bright, smiling face that you wore for us each morning! At 6:00 A.M. I never did feel full of vim and vigor —though you asked me if I did a thousand times! My hope is that someday we'll walk the streets of glory together and marvel at the awesome future that the Lord has in store for us.

Characters

The *Daystar* ....an intergalactic star cruiser

The *Daystar* Space Rangers:
   Jerusha Ericson, 15....a topflight engineer
   Raina St. Clair, 14.......the ship's communications
                    officer
   Mei-Lani Lao, 13 ....*Daystar*'s historian and linguist
   Ringo Smith, 14...........a computer wizard
   Heck Jordan, 15..........an electronics genius
   Dai Bando, 16...............known for his exceptional
                    physical abilities

The *Daystar* Officers:
   Mark Edge ....*Daystar*'s young captain
   Zeno Thrax..................the first officer
   Bronwen Llewellen ....the navigator; Dai's aunt
   Ivan Petroski...............the chief engineer
   Temple Cole ....the flight surgeon
   Tara Jaleel ....the weapons officer
   Studs Cagney ....the crew chief

Contents

1

An Unlikely Hero

The *Daystar* was within seconds of taking off. On
the bridge the crew made the final preparations
that would program the cruiser back into the stars
from spaceport. Then the liftoff thrusters began pro-
pelling the ship upward.

Dai Bando and Crew Chief Studs Cagney stood at
the engine room port, watching the growing distance
between the docking bay and the cruiser.

Dai whistled. "I wouldn't want to be caught under
the thrusters when they're fired up. That heat would
burn you to a crisp!"

"Yeah, I know," Studs replied evenly as he stared
through the portal.

Dai frowned slightly. He could tell that something
was on the crew chief's mind.

Dai had grown to like this gruff man who ran the
"grunts" on the cruiser—the workers who performed
the duties needed for ship maintenance and cargo sup-
plies. Most of these were young men eager to get into
outer space any way that they could. Others were working for passage to another star system. Either way, Studs
would get his money's worth out of them, for he worked
them hard.

Studs had thinning black hair and dark eyes. A
short man, he also had a tree-trunk muscular build and
was as strong as a bull. He had come up the hard way
in his journey through the stars. Dai was positive that
no one aboard the *Daystar* had seen as many adven-

tures in strange places as the chief—except perhaps his Aunt Bronwen. Neither talked too much about the past. One thing Dai knew for sure—no one could handle the grunts better than Studs.

Studs started to say something and then cleared his throat and began chewing his lower lip.

Dai glanced away from the bright jets of hot gases that raced out of the thrusters. "What's wrong, Chief?"

Cagney kept looking out the window. "Several years ago . . . I don't know . . . how old are you, son?"

"Sixteen."

"Well, I was just a little older than you, maybe nineteen or twenty. I was working for the spaceport on Primas Three."

"I've always wanted to visit there. I hear it's beautiful."

"No doubt about it. A lot of ships visit there every year, and they need a lot of grunts to handle the cargo and the passenger luggage." Studs placed his hands in his pockets and took a deep breath. Then he expelled the air very slowly. "I was working with a good friend of mine. It was my first job in a spaceport. He had more experience being a grunt than me. He helped me a lot."

The crew chief became quiet again.

"What happened?" Dai said softly. It didn't take much intuition to sense the pain that Studs Cagney was feeling.

"I wasn't paying attention. They'd announced that we should clear the docking bay area, but I was too busy admiring the beauty of the space liner. At the time, it was the handsomest ship I'd ever seen. It was a lot like an ocean liner in space."

Studs moved back from the portal a few inches and went on. "Anyway, I was just below the liner's starboard thruster as the ignition process began. My friend

—his name was Jim Thornton—ran at me and shoved me out of the way. At that moment the thrusters ignited. I looked back just in time to see my friend burned to ashes in a split second."

Studs took his hands out of his pockets and then traced the outline of the portal with his right index finger. "I can never look at a thruster without thinking of Jim, his smile—and his death."

Not knowing what to say, Dai remained quiet, but he placed a hand on Studs's shoulder. They continued to look out the portal until the blue atmosphere turned into star-spangled blackness.

As soon as the *Daystar* cleared the Memphis Spaceport, Captain Edge ordered, "Ringo, slowly bring the main engines on-line and increase our forward speed gradually. No sense making an ion storm over the spaceport."

Suddenly Ens. Raina St. Clair came running up to the captain, her face troubled. "Captain, there's an urgent message for you from King Denethor!"

"I'll take it in my cabin."

The captain hurried to the privacy of his cabin, switched on the view screen, and saw the tense face of the king. "Captain Edge here, Your Majesty. Is there some trouble?"

"Indeed there is, Captain!" Denethor spoke rapidly. "I hate to be the bearer of ill news, but Zaria has escaped."

"Escaped! How'd she get away?"

"I must bear the responsibility. She's not called the Queen of Darkness for nothing. She still has strange powers, and many of her followers have not given up yet. Somehow they overcame all the obstacles, killed her guards, and she's gone." He hesitated, then said, "I fear she's left the planet, Captain. We cannot find her anywhere!"

"Well, thanks for the warning, Your Majesty. We'll be alert. And you must remember that our mission to Morlandria was to keep you from being assassinated and that Zaria is the prime suspect. I suggest you triple your guard until she is apprehended."

"I've already done that, Captain. Once again, you have done your job, and I fear we have been remiss in ours. But the Lord will be with us, and may the Lord be with you on your journey."

"Thank you, Your Majesty, I appreciate that. Over and out!"

Captain Edge went to find Zeno Thrax.

Zeno was an albino, his skin white as paste. Even his eyes were colorless. He was also a fine first officer and a good friend.

"I've got bad news, Zeno. Zaria's escaped," the captain said briefly.

"That *is* bad news," the first officer said, startled. "How could that happen?"

"Nobody is quite sure. But she's loose, and the king isn't safe as long as she is."

"Shall we return to the planet?"

"No, the king is reasonably sure that she has escaped somehow from Morlandria, and he is taking very adequate precautions." Edge's eyes narrowed. "We'll radio this to base and see if they give us any orders about returning, but I don't think they will."

Aboard the P54, one of the small corvettes used by the Space Academy, Karl Bentlow and Olga Von Kemp were both pleased with their smooth takeoff.

At fifteen, Olga was one year behind Karl at the Intergalactic Space Academy. For some reason,

Commandant Marta Inch frequently sent them on important errands together. That was just fine with Olga. Any reason that would put her together with the handsome Karl was fine with her. He treated her as an equal—a rare occurrence at the Academy.

They were headed back to Earth, shooting through the blackness of space. As Karl Bentlow sat at the controls, he was pleased with the power and the maneuverability of their ship. The P54 Combat Corvette was the most modern star fighter in the Intergalactic Command.

Bentlow sat back in his command chair, studying the bridge. Like the ship itself, the bridge was circular. A three-dimensional viewer was located at the center. From this position, everyone working on the bridge had a good view. Each system console was mobile and could be positioned according to the captain's desire.

It was a magnificent ship indeed, but somehow Karl could not experience the pleasure that he had upon first assuming command. He knew why. He still could not get away from the words of Jerusha Ericson about trusting in Jesus Christ. It was so foreign to him to trust anyone that he could not put it all together.

Suddenly he was jolted by Olga's sudden and rather harsh voice.

"Have you gone to sleep, Karl? You're off course by two degrees!"

"Oh. Thanks, Olga!"

"You still daydreaming about that girl?"

Karl could not deny it and was about to change the subject. But before he could, he was frozen by another voice.

"Both of you stand absolutely still, or you will die!"

Both Karl and Olga whirled.

11

He was astonished to see the high priestess of Astarte, dressed in jet black, standing behind them. Zaria had a Neuromag trained on them, and her finger was white on the trigger.

"Don't shoot!" Olga begged. "Don't kill us!"

"I certainly will—if you don't do *exactly* as I say!"

"So you escaped," Karl said. "It won't do you much good. You'll be caught." He clenched his fists tightly.

"No, I will not be caught, and I will see the royal family dead before I'm through!" A cruel expression crossed her face, and her lips twisted with rage. "I will destroy you too, if you do not do just as I say! Now, turn around, and I will give you a new course!"

"We're going back to Earth," Karl protested.

"No, you are not going to Earth! You're going to a planet where I have many followers! We will take back Morlandria, and I will assume the throne there! I am the rightful heir to the throne of Morlandria!"

Strangely, the more Zaria's rage increased, the more her evil beauty seemed to magnify. It was a beauty that the average man could not resist. She had the kind of power over men that enticed them first to love and then to worship her. Many a strong man had come to a bad end because of her.

Now Zaria glared down menacingly at Karl with eyes that were as dark as her long hair.

Karl Bentlow had been shaken at first by the appearance of the high priestess. Ordinarily, he would have obeyed her every command, but somehow anger filled him that this woman would take over *his* ship. *What will they say at the Academy if I let a lone woman take over my ship?*

And then he saw that Zaria's attention had been caught by one of the crewmen passing by. She turned her head slightly. In that split second, Karl Bentlow made a most courageous decision.

She can't take over my ship!

He launched himself from his chair. But even as he covered the short distance between himself and Zaria, he saw that he would be too late. The muzzle of the Neuromag swung about. A light flickered, and searing pain tore through his shoulder. Clutching it, Karl dropped to the floor.

Zaria came close and held her weapon to his temple.

"One more wrong move, and you are dead!" She looked at Olga then. "All right. You will take me to Sir Richard Irons."

"Don't do it, Olga!"

Olga gave one agonizing look at Karl, struggling with the pain in his shoulder. "We've got to do it, Karl."

"Not Richard Irons! Don't do it!"

Then Karl felt the hot muzzle of the Neuromag touch his temple.

"Do you want to die?" Zaria said.

"No! Don't shoot him!" Olga cried. "Don't shoot! I'll do it! I can navigate! I'll take you anywhere you want to go!"

A satisfied smile touched the lips of the high priestess of Astarte. "I thought it would be like that," she said. "You poor fools—to think you could defeat my powers! I promise you that the *Daystar* Space Rangers will not live long, either! They will not only have me to contend with but the powers of Sir Richard Irons as well!" She laughed and gave a sweeping motion with the Neuromag. "Now, you will do what I tell you or else!"

The P54 shot through empty space under Olga's control.

13

Karl knew what would happen to them both as soon as their usefulness was over. She would kill them. There was no mercy in the Queen of Darkness.

As they passed by the stars that spangled the heavens, Karl began thinking of something Jerusha had said.

She said that Jesus is able to do all things. If He can do anything—then He has more power than this evil woman. Oddly, the thought encouraged him.

As the medical attendant bound his wound under the watchful eye of Zaria, Karl kept his own counsel. Although his wound felt like fire, his mind envisioned Jerusha, and somehow he knew he had to stand for what was right. He was supposed to call her after he landed the P54 at the Academy. He lay against the bridge bulkhead and wondered if he would ever see her again.

Zaria stood directly behind Olga Von Kemp, so close that the Neuromag touched the back of her head. She knew the girl was frightened, and it gave her pleasure to increase that fear.

"Just one point off course, and you'll be sorry! I can fly this ship myself if need be. I'll throw your worthless body out into space!" She was pleased to see the girl's hands trembling.

Then Zaria looked ahead into the blackness of space. Somewhere out there lay Sir Richard Irons, and her mind worked quickly, plotting how she and Irons together would put an end to the Space Rangers.

Then she would be the true Queen of Darkness!

2

A Return Trip

The two girls walked slowly along the broad street that ran between rows of shining buildings. They were dressed in identical uniforms. The tunic was slate gray with silver trim on the collar and above the cuffs. Close-fitting navy slacks had a silver stripe down the sides. The ensign insignia was positioned on the right sleeve, and the *Daystar* Space Ranger insignia was on the left. Each uniform was finished off with a pair of black, rubber-soled half boots.

Jerusha Ericson and Raina St. Clair had grown to be close friends. They found any excuse they could to wander away from *Daystar* together when the ship was in port.

"Jerusha, you told me we were going to visit the Astrodome ruins," Raina said. She looked skyward in exasperation. "We're going in the opposite direction! The only facility in this direction is the Space Academy!"

Jerusha tucked her hair behind her ears and pretended not to hear her friend, whose voice was getting higher and faster.

Both were attractive girls. Ensign Ericson had ash-blonde hair and dark blue eyes set in a squarish face. At five ten she was strong, athletic, and filled with exuberant health.

Raina St. Clair was only five feet three. She had an abundance of auburn hair featuring a widow's peak, and she had a slight cleft in her chin.

Both were currently on leave from the *Daystar*

and had been looking forward to some rest and recreation back here on planet Earth.

But Raina had an annoyed look in her green eyes. "Jerusha," she finally said in exasperation, "why in the world did you trick me into coming back to the Academy? I never wanted to see this place again as long as I lived, and I wouldn't think you would either!"

Jerusha and Raina, along with the other *Daystar* Space Rangers, had been expelled from the Space Academy. Commandant Marta Inch considered the whole lot of them rebellious and stubborn. In fact, though, all but one of the Rangers had been thrown out for their Christian beliefs. Only Heck Jordan had been dismissed because he seemed rebellious and stubborn. And in truth, Heck was an electronics genius and had always been tinkering with the Academy's circuit boards. Needless to say, all the Space Rangers had bad memories of the Space Academy.

Without breaking stride, Jerusha glanced down at her companion. "You're just tired after our adventure on Morlandria," she said. "You've got time lag after our long flight home."

"But why are you *doing* this?"

As the two girls approached the front entrance to the Academy and slowed their pace, Jerusha said with a worried expression, "I can't imagine why Karl hasn't contacted me. We've been back to Earth for days now, and he promised that he would. I think something must have happened to their ship. That's why I wanted to come here—to see if there's been any news about the P54. The only way I could get you to come with me was to fool you. I'm sorry. I just didn't want to come by myself!"

Raina sighed. "It *is* rather strange," she admitted. She was the *Daystar*'s communications expert. "I tried everything I could to contact their ship, but it's like they disappeared into a black hole." Raina looked at Jerusha thoughtfully. "Those two were nothing but hateful to us at the Academy. Are you really worried about them?"

"I guess I am."

"And I guess I don't see why you should be. They treated us like clowns. I really think they had something to do with us being expelled."

"No, I don't believe that. Karl's not that sort of guy!"

"But Olga's that sort of girl. Karl's always liked you, and she's dangerously jealous."

As they started up the steps, Raina said, "Do you remember some of the awful times we had? It seems like a century ago since we were here."

"Still, I don't think it was *all* bad. Remember when the P54 took us for a trip around Saturn?"

"That was exciting all right. I had no idea there were that many colors in the universe. There was no way I could have counted the planet's rings. The way the sunlight reflected off them was dazzling!"

"All in all, I wish things could have turned out different," Jerusha said. "I really wanted to be in the Intergalactic Fleet in the worst way."

"Well, we had a few good times here all right," Raina said. "But Karl and Olga played some pretty bad jokes on me. They hurt all of us badly, Jerusha."

"Yes, all of us. It's rather strange that so many of the *Daystar* crew are people who didn't make it in the Academy."

"I suppose that's all Captain Edge could get to fly his missions."

Capt. Mark Edge had done the recruiting. His older crew members had been skeptical of the young people, calling them a nursery crew, but they had proved their worth in their first mission. By now they were tested, disciplined Space Rangers.

"Notice how everybody is staring?" Jerusha asked. "It's our nonregulation uniforms."

She had no sooner spoken than a boy wearing the uniform of the Space Academy approached and said with a snide tone, "Well, if it isn't Jerusha! You come to beg to get back into the Academy?"

"Hello, Denton. I see you're still here. What's the matter? Couldn't pass your astrophysics exam?"

The cadet scowled and said roughly, "You might as well turn around and go back, you and Ragtag Raina. We've heard about you running around with that pirate, Edge."

"You're just jealous because you can't pass your exams and be assigned to a star cruiser." Jerusha smiled sweetly. "Run along now and play with your toys, while we real space fighters get on with our business."

They stood watching the fourteen-year-old stalk down the steps and toward the canteen building.

Raina said, "He always was a nasty boy. I'm surprised he hasn't failed because of his stupidity. And he never combs that mousy-looking hair of his. I swear, sometimes I thought a bird was going to land on that mess and start building a nest!"

"I think his father's on the board. They're afraid to throw him out."

"Well, I suppose our uniforms do look a little odd to them. They're so different. They're prettier, I think."

"It's a good thing Heck didn't come with us. Nothing he wears ever matches!"

"Yes, he always finds some sort of odd-colored neckerchief or jacket to go with the uniform."

They grinned as they thought of the *Daystar*'s electronics expert and his colorful outfits.

Raina said, "And to people here at the Academy, I suppose we look as ridiculous as Heck." Suddenly she said, "Jerusha, *why* are we coming to this place?"

"I've already told you. I want to find out about Karl."

Raina stopped and grabbed Jerusha's arm, turning her about. "I can't understand why you're so concerned about *Karl* all of a sudden."

Jerusha shifted her feet and looked down for a moment. When she lifted her eyes, she said seriously, "Karl's changed, Raina. He's not like he was back in the old days."

"You've said that before, but we don't really know. You have to be around someone a while before you can know whether he's really changed or not. I think you've finally fallen for Karl just because he's so good-looking."

Jerusha's face flamed. "Raina, I'm tired of you accusing me of being in love with every guy I meet! First, you said I liked Captain Edge, which is ridiculous, and now it's Karl Bentlow!"

"Well, it's true. You do get crushes on guys."

"That's absolutely ridiculous."

But Raina, whom Jerusha knew to be the kindest person on board the *Daystar*, and certainly the most devout Christian, threw up her hands. "You just can't see how you've changed, Jerusha. You've been reading too many romances!"

Jerusha glared. "All right, once in a while maybe I do have a tendency to have a crush on a boy—or somebody like Captain Edge—but this is different. Something is wrong with Karl and Olga. I sense it."

This statement caused Raina to close her mouth at once and just look at the older girl. "All right, Jerusha," she said quietly. "I'm sorry. I didn't mean to say bad things about you. If you're really worried—"

Jerusha nodded briefly, saying with a smile, "Apology accepted."

And then the two stepped up to the front entrance.

Jerusha took a deep breath. "The last time I walked through this door was the day I was kicked out of the Academy."

"I know what you mean. Look right over there." Raina pointed to a spot on the manicured lawn. "When you say you were thrown out, you were probably using figurative language. But I was actually *physically* thrown out." She nodded toward a huge white stone that was shaped like an ancient airplane and had NASA engraved on the side. "That Denton may have forgotten it, but he grabbed me, shoved me down the steps, and then gave me a push. I sat down right next to the NASA monument."

The girls looked at each other.

Finally, Jerusha smiled and put her arm around the younger girl. "Well, they can't throw us out again. If they do, we'll turn our expert martial arts skills on them."

Raina laughed out loud. "I think a Neuromag would be more effective!"

"Raina, I *know* something's not right about the P54. I need you to help me break their encryption codes. You're the expert in that area."

"I'll do what I can, but I bet we won't come within a light-year of their communications console!"

Jerusha flinched at that. But then she said, "Who knows? Maybe we'll get lucky."

The two Space Rangers walked into the large foyer of the main building of the Academy.

Jerusha looked up at the walls on both sides. Large planetary flags hung like banners across the room.

"Raina, I remember the first time I saw the flags."

"Me too!"

"I studied every one of them. Each from a different planet, each with a different history. Some of their stories are so good. They made me feel wonderful about science and the ability of mankind to reach out to the stars."

"I know. I felt the same way. But each planet has a dark side too."

Jerusha nodded her head slowly. "Unfortunately, that's very true."

"No matter how hard a person, or a country, or even a whole planet tries to have good values and morals, there is no hope for success without Jesus Christ. Greed, lust, and pride are still alive in the hearts of man. Only Jesus Christ can bring the needed changes in our lives and in our planet." Raina's convictions ran strong and deep.

Jerusha continued to look up at the colorful flags, each with its own distinctive markings. "Our God is the God of the universe. He's the Lord of the heavenly hosts, the Bible says. Raina, we can't change the whole galaxy, but at least we can help the few people the Lord leads our way. Bronwen says that we should never doubt the power of one person to change things. She calls it 'the power of one.'"

Raina turned toward Jerusha and ran her fingers through her hair. "Sometimes the darkness seems so strong, I'm afraid it causes me to take my eyes off Jesus."

Jerusha understood that. "And I'm so headstrong all the time that I forget that *His* opinion is the only one that matters." She pointed to a stairwell in the far corner. "Let's try the registrar's office first. Maybe they can give us a simple yes or no answer."

Raina responded glumly, "I think I'm going to regret this."

21

3
Aboard the P54

Her face marked with anxiety, Olga Von Kemp bent over Karl Bentlow. Her brown eyes showed a strong concern for the boy who lay against the bulkhead, his face pale.

"How do you feel, Karl?"

"Not . . . very good."

The injury that Karl had taken just as they left the planet Morlandria was not getting any better. The wound ran deep into his shoulder and was filling with fluid. Soon, his internal organs would be infected. Putting a hand on his forehead, she bit her lip for his brow was hot, and she knew he already had a fever.

He needs a doctor's care, Olga thought, but other than the med technician, there was no medical help on board the vessel that was cutting its way through the vastness of space. The P54 was one of the finest ships in the galaxy, but with Zaria, high priestess of Astarte, in control, neither Karl nor Olga had much hope.

A rough hand suddenly grabbed Olga's hair and jerked her head back, and she found herself staring into the face of Zaria. "What are you up to?"

There was not a trace of pity in that face as she looked down on the injured boy. If Karl's life were not in danger, Olga would have tried to knock out the high priestess with one blow.

Zaria seemed to sense her anger. A smile twisted her lips—she was an expert at fueling anger—and she said, "He's almost done for. You can cross him off, like it or not!"

"You can't let him die! You've got to get us to a doctor!"

"A doctor!" Zaria's laugh was hard as diamonds. "You can forget about that. When I get through with him, there'll be nothing for a doctor to recognize. Now, I've given you the course. Get about your business and leave him alone!"

As Zaria turned and stalked off, Olga leaned toward Karl quickly and whispered, "I've got a plan, Karl, and as soon as I find out exactly where we're going, I'll do something."

"What can you do?" Karl groaned. "She'd kill you if she thought you were going to betray her."

"I'm going to contact Intergalactic Command."

"She'll never let you do that. She's too sly, and she's deadly." Karl took her hand. "Don't take any chances."

For a long time Olga had longed for Karl Bentlow to take her hand, but she knew this was not a romantic gesture. He was simply weak. She said firmly, "We've got to do *something*. We're going near the Cygnus Sector, and you know what that means. Besides, she will kill us anyway when we have served her purpose."

"Yes . . . she will." Karl closed his eyes and slipped back into a state of semiconsciousness.

Olga stared at his handsome face. Even at his age, Karl looked like a starship captain. She knew he could be cruel and obnoxious sometimes, but then at other times he was full of sincerity and gentleness. She touched his brow and noted that the fever was growing worse.

Olga returned to the command chair of the P54 and analyzed their situation. She pushed a few buttons on the astronavigation console, and the three-dimensional viewer formed the Cygnus Sector in front of her. She flipped another switch, and the position of the P54 appeared, indicating that they were headed right into the heart of Denebian space—and into harm's way.

Olga had read all the stories. The Cygnus Sector, she remembered, had been colonized almost a thousand years ago. It had been a mysterious section of the cosmos, and it remained mysterious and dangerous.

The inhabitants of Cygnus were called Denebians, from the sector's giant star Deneb. They were a fierce, warlike race of humans who did not welcome visitors into their star system. In fact, those unfortunate captains who led their ships into that sector frequently were never seen again.

Zaria returned, saw the 3-D image of Cygnus, and studied Olga with a cold eye. Then she snapped, "Open communications!"

Olga did not know whether to address Zaria as "sir," which she normally would have done with a superior officer, or "ma'am," which was the old Earth style of address for an older woman. Instead, she asked, "Which code?"

"Code 457-6X."

Olga was adept at the communications systems on the P54, and her fingers flew over the keyboard. In a few seconds the screen in front of them was filled with the image of a man.

Instantly Olga recognized him. Everyone in the galaxy knew Sir Richard Irons.

Sir Richard Irons was one of the most powerful men alive. A burly man still in his thirties, Irons had dark brown hair and deep-set brown eyes with a gold tinge. He stood more than six three and was both handsome and imposing.

But Sir Richard Irons was not only a handsome

star ship commander. He was also a space pirate. He had, as many had found, a smooth manner, and his title was real—he actually was *Sir* Richard Irons. But he was a space outlaw who showed no mercy.

Irons was extremely wealthy. He had a fleet of fast cruisers manned by tough, ruthless captains. He deployed spies all over the cosmos, including the Academy and the Intergalactic Council. His aim, which he did not allow others to know at the moment, was to become head of the Council, and he would stop at nothing to accomplish this. Day by day, as he moved closer to his goal, his resolve became more steel-like.

The figure on his view screen said, "I am Queen Zaria, Sir Richard, and I have news for you."

"I know of no *Queen* Zaria!" Irons snapped. "This communication is coming from a corvette! What is your purpose?"

"I am going to the Cygnus Sector," she flared, "but I need to meet with you first!"

Irons could not conceal his irritation. How could she be so stupid as to bring a P54 anywhere near his headquarters? His voice crackled as he said, "I command you to stop where you are! I will tractor you to my headquarters!"

"I will not do that, Sir Richard," Zaria said. "I have other plans in mind."

"I've had enough of your plans! You're a failure, Zaria! You failed me on Morlandria! The Space Rangers won! I will not permit this! I insist that you come at once to my headquarters on the *Jackray* and forget about the Cygnus Sector."

"I'm not one of your flunkies, and I will not obey! I have powers that you do not appreciate, and I refuse to come to your headquarters."

Irons couldn't help but admire the beauty of the

woman who stood before him on the three-dimensional viewer. Nevertheless, her beauty was no excuse for defiance.

"The Intergalactic Command can locate your P54 with their space beacons!" Irons snapped. "You'll be in their hands!"

Since the Denebians were warlike, the Council had ordered the placement of space beacons. These were the size and shape of twentieth-century submarine torpedoes, and they carpeted space around the Cygnus Sector. They monitored all ship movements and transmitted data to Command Central. All Intergalactic Fleet vessels had special identification transponders that communicated with the space beacons. If even one Denebian warship left the Cygnus Sector, Command Central would be notified in a nanosecond.

Irons the pirate was not the kind of man who was willing to give in to anyone, especially to a woman. "If you come and join me," he said, allowing his face to become less stern, "perhaps we can work on a joint effort." He stepped closer to the viewer, and his voice was as smooth as silk. "You may have powers, but you must appreciate my own."

But the woman on the screen shook her head and said, "Forget it, Irons! You're incapable of honorable behavior. I'll not bend the knee to you or any man. I must go my own way."

"You fool!" Irons shouted. "If you go into the Cygnus Sector, the Denebians will blast you to pieces as soon as you break their space!"

"I will take my chances!"

"No one has ever been able to handle the Denebians, either legally or illegally!" Irons snapped. "You will come at once! That is my final order! Off screen!"

***

Olga saw the fury in Zaria's face.

"He treats me like a disobedient slave, and I am no one's slave!" The sorceress paced the deck. "But soon he will be begging me for forgiveness. He'll be on his knees before me."

Zaria returned to the console, then whirled and leaped over to Karl Bentlow. She grabbed his jersey and with surprising strength lifted him from the floor. "You lied to me!"

"I don't know . . . what . . . you mean." Karl could hardly speak.

"Why didn't you tell me about the beacons?"

"I'm just a cadet, Zaria," he whispered. He tried to pull loose from her grip, but she was too strong for him. "They don't tell cadets things like that."

"That's true," Olga said, coming to Karl's side. She longed to reach out and slap Zaria's face for mistreating him, but she knew that the woman's powers were formidable and that she could be struck down instantly. "There are a great many things they don't tell us about the P54 and the technology of the Intergalactic Command."

Karl seemed almost unconscious. He was muttering now, "I think . . . a rescue fleet . . . is on its way . . . to intercept us."

Suddenly Zaria reached down and gripped his head. He gasped for breath and had none to cry out with.

"Stop it! Please stop it!" Olga screamed. She seized Zaria's arm, but the dark-haired sorceress threw her back against the bulkhead. Her head struck the hard metal, and everything seemed to swim. When she regained her balance and her vision cleared, she saw Zaria's evil smile.

The high priestess was pointing a finger toward her. "You will scan for any ships in our sector. Do it now!"

"I won't," Olga said. "I won't help you anymore unless you leave Karl alone!"

Zaria's eyes glittered. It was as if a light had appeared behind them.

Olga Von Kemp willed herself to stay where she was, but somehow she found herself walking toward the scanning console. *I can't do this,* she thought. *I can't help this woman.* But she did help her. It was as if she had lost control of her own will.

Looking at the console carefully, Olga finally whispered, "There are no Intergalactic Command ships in this sector." She hesitated, then heard herself saying, "There are many beacons, though, because we are near the Cygnus Sector."

"Then I have nothing to worry about," Zaria announced to the terrified girl.

"But the Denebians are killers. They'll butcher us all!" Olga screamed.

Zaria smiled, and then her laugh filled the cabin. "The Denebians are *my* followers. They will not harm me." She pointed a finger at Olga again. "As for you two —they'll make a feast out of you—and in my honor! I can hardly wait!" She laughed again, the laugh of the insane.

And Olga suddenly understood why the Denebians were so evil. If they were worshipers of Astarte, they were as cold-blooded as the high priestess herself. Who knew the depth of evil that lurked in their hearts? Hope for rescue by Intergalactic Command faded. Her heart sank.

Then, as she turned back to the console, she noticed a small blip enter their zone from the neighboring Pegasus Sector. Quickly she glanced over her shoulder and saw that Zaria was not watching. She touched a few keys, and the scanner identified the ship as the *Jackray*.

So that's where Sir Richard Irons has his head-quarters, she thought.

Hugging the secret in her mind, Olga wondered how she could use this knowledge to her advantage and to Karl's. The high priestess did seem to sense things, but she hoped that Zaria's powers did not include true mind reading.

Leaving the scanner console, she went back to Karl.

At first, he appeared unconscious. He lay on his back. His limbs twitched as if he were having some terrible nightmare.

"I just saw the *Jackray* on the screen, Karl," she whispered. "I think it will intercept us soon." But she grimaced at the possibility that Zaria's powers were greater than anyone imagined. "Maybe they'll rescue us."

Karl's eyes opened, and his lips twisted with pain. "That'll do us . . . no good. That's Richard Irons's . . . ship. It'll be like . . . jumping from the frying pan . . . into the fire."

And then Karl seemed to slip back into a coma and could hear no more.

Olga's fear for her friend magnified several times over as she watched his face turn even paler. She thought, *Karl needs a doctor, and he needs one now.*

4

Troubles on the *Daystar*

The sick bay of the *Daystar* was the private domain of Dr. Temple Cole. It was not as large as the arrangement she was used to aboard a Magnum Deep Space Cruiser, but the doctor found this smaller sick bay more to her liking. She had helped design it, and it was laid out in a no-nonsense manner.

Instead of the normal medical staff of thirty, she had this sick bay all to herself. Being by herself was what she needed right now, she thought, although she didn't mind the occasional visit from crew members. They made her think of problems other than her own.

The treatment area was ten feet square. Titanium cabinets lined three walls. Her office space was against the fourth. Every instrument was easily within her reach. She prided herself on having procured the latest medical technology when *Daystar* was refitted.

Sitting on a black Dernof leather chair, Dr. Cole studied the attractive girl before her.

The doctor herself, at the age of twenty-seven, was an attractive woman. She had strawberry blonde hair cut short—it was very curly despite all her efforts to curb it. She was wearing a dark blue dress that accented her violet eyes. She had been off duty when Mei-Lani had called her and asked to meet with her in the sick bay.

Temple Cole was a woman who kept herself very private. Her one secret was that, despite her determination not to fall in love again, she felt herself drawn to

31

Mark Edge, the handsome captain who commanded the *Daystar*. Even now, she found herself thinking of him.

With an effort of will she forced her mind back and away from the tall captain and put her attention on Mei-Lani Lao, the cruiser's historian and linguist. "What can I do for you, Mei-Lani?" she asked quietly.

The girl twisted uncomfortably. She was thirteen years old and had the black hair and brown eyes of most Orientals. She was barely more than five feet and weighed less than a hundred pounds. Nevertheless, in that small skull of hers was a tremendous brain. She read constantly and appeared never to forget anything. She seemed to know a lot of the history of the galaxy. Her chief value to the *Daystar* was that she could learn languages unbelievably fast.

"I wanted to talk to you about—"

Seeing the girl's face flush, Dr. Cole asked, "What is it? Are you sick, Mei-Lani?"

"Yes—I mean no." Flustered, Mei-Lani dropped her head and bit her lip. She was obviously embarrassed. Finally, she lifted her head and met Dr. Cole's eyes, whispering, "It's—it's my complexion."

With another effort of will, Temple kept back the smile that leaped to her lips. She said very calmly, "Mei-Lani, this kind of circumstance is very frustrating for a doctor sometimes. I've been waiting for you to come to me with your problem, but you never have."

"I was embarrassed."

"Why should you be embarrassed?" Dr. Cole smiled and leaned forward. "You're at the age when many young people have complexion problems."

"Not my people."

For the first time Temple realized that what Mei-Lani was saying was true. It had escaped her, but now —as she thought about it—she realized that very few

Orientals did have complexion problems. *I wonder why that is?* she thought next.

An answer popped into her head. *Perhaps it's partly their lifestyle. They are very hygienic. If teenagers would watch their diets and wash their faces more, complexion problems might lessen.* But aloud she said, "That's probably true, and all the more reason why you're embarrassed about it."

Mei-Lani's face was vulnerable. "Please, Dr. Cole, can you do something for me?"

"Mei-Lani, a thing like this is very frustrating for a doctor. Medicine has come a long way. We can cure thousands of diseases, close wounds without stitches, have even learned to repair broken bones in seconds."

"Then you ought to be able to do something about these pimples!"

"Well, the truth is, despite all of our advances in science," Temple said with a frown on her face, "there are two things we haven't learned to do."

"What two things?"

"We haven't found a cure for the common cold— or for pimples." She saw disappointment sweep across Mei-Lani's face and said then, "You know, this may be a very temporary thing. It may go away of itself, provided we structure your diet appropriately. And I do have a special soap that you can use."

"But, Doctor, I can't wait for it to go away by itself!"

Sighing deeply, Temple rose to her feet. She opened a cabinet door and took out what appeared to be a small, cordless red lamp. It looked somewhat like a hair dryer.

"What is it?" Mei-Lani asked.

"It's what we call a Neutrino Dermal Enhansor. I picked it up on Morlandria on our last mission."

"What does it do?"

Cole held out the small lamp and demonstrated. "Well, you set the device on the table—like this—and adjust it so that the light beam points at your face. See, here's the switch. You turn it on for thirty seconds."

"But what will it do?"

"It will give you a facial. It removes facial hair, bacteria, and dead skin."

"Will it help me, though?"

"That I can't promise, Mei-Lani, but I think you have a great chance for success using this device in combination with a good diet and this special soap." Cole paused for a moment. "You know, Raina St. Clair says that sometimes God gives us problems to bear just to make us better people. But you'll have to talk to her about that. She's the one who knows the Bible better than the rest around here. I just remember she told me one time that God did such things. I know we don't like bad things to happen, but she quoted me something from the Bible. Let's see—how did it go?" Temple thought for a few seconds, frowning. Then she nodded. "It went something like—everything really works out for the benefit of the people who love the Lord. Something along that line. Did you ever hear that?"

"Yes, of course, but I didn't think it had anything to do with anything as small as a complexion problem!"

Temple went over suddenly and sat down beside the girl. She put her arm around her, feeling quite motherly. "Our problems are always important to us, even if they are small to other people. Right now this is a very, very big thing in your life, Mei-Lani. It's true of all young people. I can remember when I was your age —I had the same problem."

With amazement, Mei-Lani looked at the doctor's flawless peaches-and-cream complexion. "*You* had a complexion problem?"

"Yes, I did, and I wanted to die. I thought it would never go away, but it did."

As the two sat there, Temple Cole found herself taking great pleasure in talking to the girl. Mei-Lani was so small and vulnerable that it was as if she had a daughter. She thought of ways to encourage her, finally saying, "One way or another this will pass away."

"Thank you, Dr. Cole."

"Be sure you leave this lamp on only for thirty seconds," she said as Mei-Lani rose to depart.

"Is it dangerous?"

"No, it emits a very low-powered beam. All the same, that will be plenty for you."

"Thank you, Doctor," she said again and looked up shyly. "You know, I can barely remember my mother. I hope it doesn't insult you, and I know you're young, but really it's almost like having a mother again."

Temple Cole was touched. She reached out and drew the girl to her, kissed her on the cheek, and said, "Come and talk to me about anything, Mei-Lani. Anytime. I'd be honored."

She watched as the girl left the sick bay and suddenly said aloud, "I've missed a lot by not having a family."

Contessa, the enormous black German shepherd, was asleep in a corner of the exercise room. She belonged to Ranger Jerusha Ericson and had been bred for strength and intelligence. She could follow any track through any territory. When she ran down her prey, her crushing jaws would hold whatever it was until help came.

Capt. Mark Edge, who despised dogs, had become an idol to Contessa. More than once she had placed her huge paws on his chest and licked his face while he shouted for help. Now the sleeping dog trembled. Perhaps she was dreaming of the captain.

The exercise room itself was filled with thumps and grunts of effort. Lt. Tara Jaleel, weapons officer of the *Daystar*, was having a bout with Dai Bando, the oldest of the Space Rangers.

Tara Jaleel was almost six feet tall. She had fierce features. She loved battle of any kind. She was an expert at Jai-Kando and was able to overwhelm any opposition among the crew of the ship—any except Dai Bando.

Dai alone among the Space Rangers had little technical ability. The others were all close to being geniuses at engineering, communications, or computers, but Dai Bando had none of this.

What he did have was tremendous physical skill. He had strength, agility, and speed almost beyond belief. Now, as he circled the weapons officer, he seemed totally relaxed. A gentle smile was on his lips. He was of Welsh blood. He had black hair and black eyes, and two prominent dimples showed when he smiled. At five eleven and one hundred seventy-five pounds, he had the perfect build for most athletic endeavors.

Tara Jaleel appeared frustrated again. No matter how hard she tried, she was never able to defeat this young man. As fast as she was, no matter how rapidly her hand shot out, Dai always moved slightly faster, causing her to miss. He was slipperier than an eel, and she had never once managed to get a good grip on him.

Over in a corner, two other Space Rangers were watching the bout. One was Ringo Smith.

Ringo hated physical battles of any kind, for he was not good at them. He briefly fingered the medallion that hung around his neck. It had a hawk or falcon on one side and the profile of a strong-looking man on the other side. He glanced at the motto on the medallion. It was in some exotic language that not even Mei-Lani Lao could read.

Actually Ringo did not feel comfortable on the *Daystar.* He felt insecure. As he sat there, he thought suddenly of Raina St. Clair, with whom he fancied himself desperately in love. Then his glance went back to the handsome boy circling Tara Jaleel. He knew Raina liked Dai Bando a great deal.

"Look at that!" The overweight red-haired boy at his side reached into his pocket and pulled out a piece of chocolate, then popped it into his mouth. He laughed softly. "I always like to see Lieutenant Jaleel take her licks from Dai. Look at that! She can't lay a hand on him!"

Heck Jordan was a genius in electronics, but he did have several rather glaring flaws. Aside from being overweight, his clothes never matched. Then, being tremendously egotistical, he was convinced that all girls were in love with him. Insults rolled off him like water off the hide of a crocodile. To most of his shipmates, Heck defined the meaning of extreme selfishness. The saddest flaw in Heck was that he was the only one of the Space Rangers who was not a Christian.

As the two boys continued to watch, Ringo said, "Lieutenant Jaleel's tough, but she'll never whip Dai."

"She'll whip *us*, though," Heck said. "I dread every one of these sessions."

"Well, let's you and I have our bout." Ringo sighed.

The boys got to their feet and began circling each other. Neither one of them was good at martial arts. Both of them hated it thoroughly, but Lieutenant Jaleel insisted that they go through the exercise. As they moved around in a circle, their loose-fitting outfits swished against their legs.

37

Ringo made the first move. His hand shot out, and he grabbed Heck by the arm. His grip barely reached around Heck's thick forearm. Ringo twisted his body and brought up Heck's arm and tried to throw him over his shoulder.

It was like trying to throw a big rock!

Ringo grunted and strained, but still Heck didn't move. Looking over his shoulder, Ringo said, "Sparring with you is like trying to spar with a beached whale!"

"I knew my eating was good for something." Heck laughed, reached into his pocket, and pulled forth an unwrapped candy bar. He bit off half of it in one bite and chewed hungrily. "I bet very few people can throw me because of my weight."

Unfortunately, Lieutenant Jaleel heard this remark. She was probably angry that she had not been able to touch Dai Bando. In any case, upon hearing Heck's bragging, she came up behind him, and her hands suddenly closed on his neck.

Ringo watched in amazement. The overweight boy suddenly flew upward, cartwheeled in the air, and crashed against the far wall, where he slid down to the floor.

Jaleel then stormed out of the exercise room.

Dai and Ringo rushed over to Heck.

"Are you all right, Heck?" Dai said anxiously.

"I don't know. What did that witch do to me?"

"I guess she proved you don't know what you're talking about." Ringo grinned. "You had just said that nobody could throw you, and then she tosses you like you were a Ping-Pong ball."

"She caught me off guard," Heck mumbled. He still seemed in a daze. He looked up at Dai and said sweetly, "Raina, is that you, honey? I knew you would see things my way."

Dai, who smiled often but laughed rarely, suddenly found this amusing. "If I look like Raina to you, I think you're unconscious."

"Wake up, Heck!" Ringo said.

Contessa, who must have awakened when Heck hit the wall, suddenly leaped to her feet and bounded in their direction.

Dai spotted her coming. He yanked Ringo out of the way at the last second, and the huge black dog landed right on top of Heck.

"Get her off of me! Get her off!" he screamed.

Contessa, however, would not be moved. She put her full weight on Heck's pudgy body. Then the dog reached out and snatched the remaining half candy bar from his hand. Whirling, she trotted out the exercise room door.

Heck sat up slowly and stared after her. "Why is everyone always picking on me?" he moaned.

"You bring it on yourself," Ringo said, smiling. He looked at Dai. "Not usually much humor in these sessions for me."

"Me, either!" Heck said, still looking after Contessa.

Dai shook his head. He looked at his two friends as though he thought they were rather frivolous. "Come on," he said, "I think we'd better take showers and get down to the chow hall."

As the three left the exercise room, Heck was saying loudly, "I've got to stop and pick up some more candy bars. I'm running out of food!"

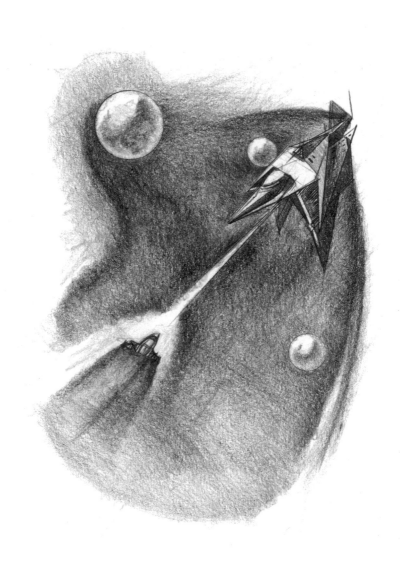

5

The *Jackray* Takes Over

Commandant Winona Lee looked more like a gentle grandmother than the highest authority of the Intergalactic Council.

A small woman with gray hair and alert gray eyes, she wore the official uniform of the Council. A dark green military-style jacket had golden trim decorating each sleeve and the epaulets on her shoulders. The jacket buttoned up to the collar. Her pants were the same dark green with a wide golden stripe positioned on the outside of each leg. The insignia of the Intergalactic Council was affixed to her jacket's right front pocket. Dark green shoes made of a velvetlike material completed her outfit.

"What is your analysis of our problem, Captain Pursey?" she asked, studying the man who sat across from her.

Capt. Miles Pursey, an older man, had dark, very tanned skin, black hair, and a small mustache. He was no more than medium size, but there was a strength about him that a first officer had to have in order to serve Commandant Winona Lee.

Pursey hesitated for a moment, and his eyes considered the papers that the two had been going over. Their meeting had been going on for more than two hours, and he was stiff with inactivity. It irritated him that the commandant showed no strain, but he had learned long ago that this woman had the character and strength of steel instead of flesh and blood.

"I think we're going to have to address the problem of Sir Richard Irons, Commandant."

"Ah, yes, his name does come up rather often, doesn't it?"

"Indeed it does. All our intelligence-gathering agencies believe he is involved with every significant organization in the galaxy. Data has indicated for some time that his plan is to rule over the Council." Pursey leaned toward her, his eyes intent. "He's gotten too big for his britches, if you'll pardon an old Earth expression."

Commandant Lee smiled gently. "I have heard it before. It is a remark that Irons would not appreciate."

"I don't give a nova whether he appreciates it or not! We've got to do something about the man. Every time we attempt to accomplish anything, *he's* in the way. How does he get by with it?"

"He has money. That's the secret. Did you know in the Bible there's a Scripture that says that money will buy anything?" She smiled at him.

Pursey, who knew the Bible, shook his head violently. "I don't believe that, and neither do you, Commandant!"

"Yes, I do, and so will you if you think about it. Listen as I quote a verse: 'Money is the answer to—' she hesitated, then continued with emphasis '—every-*thing.'* Do you see?"

"Why . . . yes, I believe I do," Pursey said. He thought about that, then added, "If you have money enough, you can buy any *thing.* Any suit, any home, any vehicle, any spaceship—if you have money."

"Yes, that's what it means. It won't buy peace, because peace is not a thing. It won't buy righteousness or goodness or forgiveness or eternal life, because those are not *things.* But money will buy things, and Sir Richard Irons has more wealth, I suppose, than any other man in the galaxy."

"Something's got to be done!" Pursey said.

"What would you propose, Captain? Have him assassinated?"

"Well, that has been suggested, but, of course, we couldn't do that. But look here—" Pursey reached over and shuffled through the reports lying on the table between them. "This business on Morlandria—Captain Edge and his Space Rangers were successful. That seems to be one time that Sir Richard Irons didn't get what he wanted."

"I'm worried about that situation, Captain Pursey."

"How is that, Commandant?"

"Two things. First, knowing Sir Richard, I have no doubt that he will try to take revenge on the *Daystar* crew. That frightens me. And then there is that woman, Zaria. The 'Queen of Darkness,' as she likes to call herself. She's a danger to the whole galaxy."

"You believe her to be *that* dangerous?" Pursey was again surprised. He leaned back and examined the commandant's face. She was an astute judge of character, he knew, and seldom seemed to be wrong. "I hadn't thought a high priestess on a remote planet was that important."

"Sir Richard Irons thinks so," Commandant Lee said quietly. "The woman has evil powers that are tremendous, far beyond the power of a neutron particle beam. What if those two join forces—she and Irons?" The commandant frowned. "They could create havoc if they decide to become team players. I can only hope that both of them are too self-important to share power with anyone else."

"Well, no one's been able to find her yet on the planet."

"She's not there, Captain," Commandant Lee said confidently. "She would have been found if she were."

"As long as we're talking about finding things, I might as well brief you on another problem."

"Out with it."

"Well, I'm concerned about one of our P54s. It's supposed to have been back here by now."

"That's the one flown by Bentlow and Kemp, the two ensigns."

"Yes, it is, and while we're at it," Captain Pursey said, "I think Commander Inch exceeded her authority in letting two ensigns take a ship like that out alone."

"I agree with you."

"But . . . but then, why didn't you stop her, Commandant?"

"Because I am not omnipotent. I'm not even omnipotent within the Intergalactic Council. Marta Inch has friends in high places, and they overrode my protest."

"Well, they may think differently if that ship is lost! You know what that thing cost."

"I know very well, but I'm more concerned about the two ensigns that are on it."

"Do you know them?"

"I know all of our ensigns. Bentlow and Kemp are not our finest, but they are ours." She leaned back and said, "Our finest were thrown out of the Academy by Inch. They are now the *Daystar* Space Rangers."

The captain knew that this, indeed, was the history of the Space Rangers. When the head of the Academy took a dislike to Jerusha Ericson and the others, she had had them put out by force. That was when Mark Edge recruited them for duty on board the *Daystar.*

"Evil people may have power for a while, Captain Pursey, but it does not last. One day Marta Inch will make a mistake. I'm biding my time until she falls into one of her own traps."

A light suddenly blinked overhead, and Commandant Lee said, "Come in!"

The two turned toward the door as Maj. Matt Moyer, second in command of Commandant Lee's flagship, entered.

"What is it, Major?"

Matt Moyer, at the age of forty-five, was a trim and fit officer with muscular arms and shoulders. "We've had a report, Commandant. One of our space beacons has picked up a P54's homing signal."

Instantly Pursey said, "That has to be the one with Bentlow and Kemp on it—coming from Morlandria."

"I'm glad to hear it. We've been worried about them, Major Moyer."

"Yes, Commandant, but there may be a problem. There are consistently *three* life-forms on the P54 bridge."

Silence fell over the room. Everyone, Pursey thought, was probably thinking the same thing.

It was Commandant Lee who said, "I think we all know who that third life-form is, don't we, gentlemen?"

"It has to be the missing Zaria. She's commandeered that ship somehow and forced our ensigns to take her aboard. That's how she made her escape."

At once Lee said, "Captain Pursey, dispatch a Magnum Deep Space Cruiser to that P54 at once!"

"Sir, that may be difficult," Major Moyer said.

"Why would that be difficult, Major?"

"Because it's almost in the Cygnus Sector, sir."

Once again silence fell over the room.

Commandant Lee finally said, "If that P54 gets near Cygnus, the Denebians will destroy it without mercy! I'm surprised that they haven't already been turned into asteroid ash!"

* * *

To Olga Von Kemp, everything in life had turned into a nightmare. As she continued to pilot the P54 closer to the Cygnus Sector, she kept her eyes focused on the 3-D video display. The *Jackray*, she saw, was rapidly approaching their position. She feared what might happen to them once they were transferred to Irons's cruiser.

Then, just as the last little drop of hope poised itself to fall from her, another small blip appeared on the screen. She hit a few more keys, and the scanner identified the new ship as a Magnum Deep Space Cruiser listed under the name *Cromwell*. Feeling as if she could jump ten feet high, Olga smothered her excitement to keep from drawing the attention of Zaria, who was dozing across the cabin.

Without opening her eyes, however, the priestess said bitingly, "Just relax! That Intergalactic ship is too far away to be of any use to us now. The *Jackray* will be here in a moment." She opened her eyes slightly. "And if Irons wants a fight, I'll give him one he won't forget."

Just then a tractor beam latched onto the P54 and began drawing the smaller ship toward the gigantic hull of the *Jackray*. For some reason, the P54 was not being pulled onto the *Jackray*'s flight deck.

Olga knelt by Karl, who was only semiconscious.

"Karl, can you hear me?" she whispered. "The *Jackray*'s got us in a tractor beam, and I can hear them opening the airlock."

"We're done for," he answered as he grimaced in pain.

"The *Cromwell* is coming, but it's over two parsecs away."

"We'll either be dead . . . or long gone . . . by the

time she arrives," Karl murmured, then seemed to slip away into unconsciousness.

She looked toward Zaria then and stared.

The high priestess stood directly in front of the door to the bridge. Strange green light was emanating from the woman like something that was alive. What was she going to do?

Olga knew that the woman must use enough force to vanquish her attackers, but she must not use so much that she destroyed the P54.

At that moment there was the sound of several men outside the bridge door.

"Open this door—or else!" they ordered.

Zaria stood motionless, ready to strike as soon as the door opened.

"Help!" Olga called out. "We've got an injured man in here! We need medical attention!"

Zaria turned her eyes toward Olga and gave her a "you better back off" look.

Olga understood perfectly and kept her mouth shut.

Just as the door cracked open, Zaria raised a hand. Swirling green gas shot toward the portal like a whirlwind, twisting the door frame out of shape. That propelled the door against the six men behind it, smashing them against the ship's bulkhead. Then another half dozen of Irons's men quickly entered the bridge. Zaria managed to bring her power to bear on two of them, just before a third man seized her.

She began to call upon her dark powers for help, but the man clapped a hand over her mouth. "Grab her arms and tie them behind her!" he shouted. "She can't use her power if she's bound and gagged. Move quickly!"

With a muffled scream, Zaria managed to get one arm free, but Olga jumped up and seized it. Irons's men took Zaria's arms then and handcuffed them behind her. Both silenced and bound, she had no way to conjure up help. Even as Zaria struggled, the green glow that surrounded her started to fade. She had obviously expended all her power. Soon she would be as helpless as Karl and Olga.

As the men from the *Jackray* escorted Zaria off the ship, Olga saw her chance and raced to the control console. She entered a message for the *Cromwell*, then programmed the P54 shields to come up as soon as she and Karl exited. The P54 scanners would pick up their identification bands as they left the ship. Olga was hoping the *Cromwell* would get her message and rescue them before they reached the Cygnus Sector.

"OK, you two—it's your turn now!"

Olga turned to see two gorilla-like men approaching. "We were Zaria's prisoners! My friend is unconscious. He has a bad wound. He needs emergency medical attention."

The two men looked at each other, then laughed. One of them took Olga by the arm, as the other one picked up Karl from the floor.

The man who led Olga away said, "Don't worry, missy. Your man will get all the attention he needs."

Both men again laughed loudly as Olga and Karl were taken off the P54.

Olga feared for their lives.

6

"What Am I Missing?"

The New Houston Spaceport was one of the most impressive installations in the entire galaxy. Solid white from top to bottom, this space port was more than five miles long, two miles high, and varied in width from one mile at its narrowest to ten miles at its widest.

Docking ports for all sizes of spacecraft honeycombed the complete exterior of the facility. Each docking port had its own antigravity runway that supported the weight of its ship. Gravity for onboard activities was provided for by each vessel's gravitational arrays. This feature allowed many ships to use the docking ports without fear of building collapse. Magnetic shuttles moved passengers and cargo from ship to ship, using top-of-the-line computers.

Capt. Mark Edge walked slowly around the *Daystar*, his eyes intent as he took in the damage. Edge was a strong-looking young man, blond with blue gray eyes and handsome features. He looked rather like an old-time Viking. In effect, he *was* somewhat that type. One who was familiar with the old movies from Earth had once described him as a Han Solo type from the old *Star Wars* films.

"It doesn't look too bad, Bronwen," he remarked to his companion. "I was afraid the damage would be worse."

An older woman, Bronwen Llewellen was not the typical space fleet officer, although she had been one for years. She was still vigorous-looking although small. Her silver hair caught the sunlight as she turned her dark blue eyes on Captain Edge, saying with a slight smile, "You worry about this ship as if it were a wife."

The remark amused him. "Wives are a lot more trouble than the *Daystar*," he remarked.

"You're cynical, Mark."

"The school of hard experience."

His navigator continued to study him.

He knew she had been navigating through the stars for most of her life. She had taken ships through some of the roughest nebulae and concentrated star clusters known in the galaxy. Her reputation had made her a living, breathing pioneer of space flight—a legendary navigator as well as the aunt of Dai Bando. Her Christian ethics were strong beyond belief, and Mark had found quickly that she had valuable insights. She seemed to know what was going on inside people.

Now her smile was gentle, and she said, "You're not as tough as you like to make out."

Edge returned her smile. "No, beneath this hard exterior I'm just a cream puff."

He had had reservations about taking an older woman aboard a fighting spacecraft, but more than once he'd had occasion to be grateful for Bronwen's presence. She had no official standing as a counselor, but whenever Edge had problems with his crew, he sooner or later found his way to her cabin to pour out his troubles.

"Captain, I've got a report!"

The captain turned to Ivan Petroski, the chief engineer of the *Daystar*.

Petroski was no more than four and one-half feet tall, but he was well proportioned. He had brown eyes, thick brown hair, and very sharp features. All his people on the planet Bellinka Two were to his scale.

"What's up, Chief?"

Petroski rattled off a list of minor problems and then said, "I've had Studs Cagney and his crew working triple shifts, though, so everything's all right. We'll get finished."

"Well, Studs is a disagreeable grump sometimes, but he's one of the best crew chiefs I've ever seen—as long as he stays sober. Thank heavens, he's on some sort of religious kick right now, which helps a lot."

"It's more than that, Mark," Bronwen put in quickly. "Studs is seeking after God, and I believe he's going to find Him soon."

Such remarks always disturbed the captain. He shifted uncomfortably, then turned his attention back to Petroski. "Chief, I want you to go over everything twice and then do it again. Make this ship perfect."

"Nothing's perfect" —Petroski grinned "—except me, Captain. But I'll see what I can do."

"Nothing wrong with his ego, is there?" Edge asked wryly. "He's got as much as Heck Jordan."

"Sometimes people that boast a lot are covering up something. Usually something deep down in their souls."

"Well, I don't think those two are the least bit concerned about their souls. If they're covering up anything, it's probably so deep down they don't know what it is anymore." Mark pushed a cargo bin out of the way. "Ivan and Heck are two of the most troubled men on the ship. Sometimes I just give up hope that they'll ever change!"

"No, you don't really think that, Mark. Heck has his problems, a great number of them, but deep down there's a fine young man just begging to get loose. As

51

for Ivan, he just hasn't been knocked flat on his back yet. Nobody who hasn't been rendered helpless by some kind of circumstance is really complete."

Mark Edge stared at his navigator. "Then I must be complete. I've been knocked down enough."

"I don't think so. You haven't hit bottom yet. That's the reason you're running from God. You think you're able to handle anything that comes your way." Bronwen looked him directly in the eye. "One of these days, Mark, life will hand you something you can't handle, strong as you are. That's when you'll look to God."

Edge had no answer for this. He continued his inspection of the *Daystar* in silence.

When they had reached the bow of the ship, he asked abruptly, "Are you all right, Bronwen?"

"Me? Why, yes!"

"You sure?" He pressed the question closely. His eyes were concerned as he studied her face. It showed thin lines of strain even now. "Your battle with that witch Zaria in the Shrine of Ugarit must have taken something out of you. It about drained me, and I didn't do anything."

Bronwen found this confession rather odd coming from Mark Edge, who rarely confessed he was unable to handle things. "I must admit," she said slowly—she bit her lower lip—"I have no desire to do any more battle with Zaria. I'm usually pretty sure about people, Mark, but I found myself wondering if Zaria was even human. She has such evil power, I thought maybe she was a demon in human form."

"I'll agree to that!" Captain Edge grunted. "I hope we don't run into her again."

"You can save your hopes, for we will."

Edge reached out and gripped her shoulder. "And you're certain about that, aren't you, Bronwen?"

"Absolutely certain!"

"How do you *know* these things? It always gives me the willies."

She smiled. "What are the willies?"

"I mean," Mark said, "it makes me uneasy. People aren't supposed to know what's going to happen."

"Most of the time I have no more idea about what a day or a month will bring than you or anyone else. But sometimes I do . . . sense . . . that something particular will happen. It's been that way ever since I was a child." Her eyes were grave, and she shook her head. "It's no pleasure, I can assure you."

"But you feel that we will meet Zaria again?"

"Yes, and at the risk of being accused of preaching at you, Mark, if you don't have any spiritual armor, she may destroy you."

He said, "Let's go have something to drink in my quarters."

"All right, Captain."

The two made their way to the ship's front entry hatch.

The navigator ran her fingers along the railing as they neared the front gangway. "Mark, I have to give you credit for your new design features on *Daystar*. She is such a beauty. I've always liked the delta wing design. On more than one occasion I've been navigating through a nebula and have had the bottom fall out from under the ship. Nebulas are so unpredictable. You never know when you'll hit a cyclonic air pocket. Without wings, it seems the ship plummets forever, but the delta wing design provides lift and maneuverability."

"I'm surprised they still use the same old designs." Edge looked toward the *Daystar*'s tail section. "I can maneuver in places the Magnum Deep Space Cruisers

53

could never go—even places Irons's *Jackray* can't go, and he has the best ship money can buy!"

"What about the P54 combat corvettes?" she asked.

"I'll have to admit the new crescent-shape design of the hull provides plenty of lift. They're fast and agile, and I also have to admit that the P54 could fly circles around *Daystar*. But they have one flaw."

"What's that?"

"They're powered only by Mark Four Star Drive engines. The Mark Fours are dependable and real workhorses, but we have the new Mark Five engines. And thanks to our genius Rangers, there's not a ship in the galaxy that can keep up with us."

"So the Space Rangers have been of *some* use, haven't they?"

"More than I ever thought possible. They've given the *Daystar* 831-B enhanced Star Drive engines, enhanced scanners, enhanced computers, and enhanced weapons. In fact, Jerusha and Heck have been working on increasing our shield strength. I can't even begin to understand some of their modifications. Their craftsmanship is excellent. Plus—with maybe the exception of Heck—they're great kids and very pleasant shipmates."

"Heck *is* different from the others. Remember, the others are Christians. Heck will come along eventually. I hear he's the genius for most of the new computer circuit boards."

"I am impressed with his abilities. I can't think of anyone else who has the expertise that Heck does with component level electronics, especially at only fifteen. The problem with Heck is that I don't think I can trust him. He doesn't know that I know, but he's been slowly draining my supply of tridium crystals. Just one of those could make him a very rich young man."

"Are you certain it's Heck? How many are missing so far?"

"He's the only one with access other than me. When we left Makon, I had just over one hundred in the locker on the bridge. Now there are ninety left."

"What are you going to do?" Bronwen asked seriously. She seemed to find it difficult to believe that Heck Jordan could be a common thief.

"Nothing—right now. I need him too much. And I have to actually catch him in the act. You'd better pray we're not in space. I'll throw him out the cargo hatch if he's guilty," Edge said with a grim look.

They walked up to the entry to his quarters, and the door opened like the lens of a camera.

When they were inside, he asked, "What would you like?"

"I'd like some of that melon juice that we brought back from Morlandria. It's the most delicious drink I ever tasted."

"I'll have some, too." He walked over to the pantry area and took from the cooler two bottles of juice, which was pink with small red chunks of melon floating in it. Edge handed a bottle to Bronwen, who smiled in expectation of its wonderful taste.

They sat down on the soft Dernof leather couch, and both started sipping the melon juice.

The captain was quiet for a while, apparently so quiet that finally Bronwen was moved to ask, "What's the trouble, Mark?"

A brief smile touched Edge's lips, and he shook his head. "No sense trying to hide things from you. Well, I'll admit I have been thinking a lot lately."

He took another sip of the melon juice, then gave her a direct look. "Ever since the first mission, when the Rangers came on board and we went to Makon, I've been seeing things that I can't understand. I don't know if it's God, luck, science, or human ingenuity, but so many times when it looked as if all were lost, things would happen."

Bronwen sat quietly, her hands folded, listening.

He finally ran down. "Try to explain it to me, Bronwen, and remember I'm just a simple fellow. Just a poor, dim-witted pilot."

"No, you're much more than that, Mark. But you must understand, first, that I believe God is behind all good things. The Scripture says that every good and perfect gift comes down from the Father above. Do you believe that?"

Edge shifted uncomfortably and turned the crystal bottle around in his large hands. "I don't know if I do or not." He looked around the cabin. "I always thought *I* built the *Daystar.* Are you telling me now that God built it?"

"I think that God used you to build the *Daystar.* And He's used the *Daystar* to accomplish good things."

"But I've never been a believer, Bronwen. Why would He use a guy like me?"

"I don't know the mind of God, and no one else does. All I know is He does use all sorts of people to accomplish His plans. He created every person for a purpose. He even used a man called Judas, a betrayer, to bring Jesus to the cross."

"I've never understood that part of the Bible. But then, again, I can't understand most of what that Book is about. I wind up tossing it down."

"There's much in the Bible I don't understand, either, Mark," Bronwen said. "But I believe it because the Bible says it's true."

"You're like Jerusha, Raina, and Mei-Lani. The whole bunch of you spend hours talking about the

Bible with each other and with anyone else who'll listen to you. But . . . Bronwen, I'll let you in on a secret—"

"What's that?"

"Jerusha was talking one day about how the eyes are the windows to the soul." Edge took a quick sip of juice.

The navigator remained quiet.

Edge looked at her cautiously but then continued. "Not being able to get her words out of my head, I started looking at people's eyes. She . . . I mean, she was exactly right. The ones who claim to know Jesus have a different look from anyone else on the ship. I thought Tara would have light in her eyes because of her obsessive devotion to that six-armed statue of Shiva she worships."

He paused, trying to figure out how to say what was on his heart. "After I studied everyone's eyes, I decided to look in the mirror at mine."

"And . . ."

Edge rubbed his chin with his left hand. He turned to look directly at Bronwen, his blue gray eyes wide. "I've always had girls tell me I have nice eyes . . ."

"Tell me what you're really trying to say, Mark."

"When I looked in the mirror . . . there was no light in *my* eyes, either." He looked down at his half-empty bottle of melon juice. "I guess I'm lucky they look nice, but they don't have in them what's in yours, Bronwen. I see contented light in your eyes and Jerusha's and the rest . . ."

"You've made a very important discovery! One that a lot of people never understand."

"The trouble is—I've asked God for that light to be in my eyes, too. But, nothing happens."

"There's more to it than that, Mark. Give yourself a little time. I know God is working in your life. He's drawing you to Himself slowly, a little bit at a time."

"I'm glad I have you to talk to. I can't really talk to anyone else about this. I want to talk to Temple about it, but she's . . . I don't know . . . hesitant or something." Edge set his bottle on the table in front of him.

The navigator leaned forward. "Temple is still on the way herself right now. She's in the midst of one of God's healing processes—and although she doesn't know it, God is helping her too."

"Is she talking to you about what's troubling her?" Edge picked up the bottle, swished around the contents inside of it, and drank some.

"No, she isn't—but God is." Bronwen smiled.

The two sat in the captain's cabin for a long time, Mark Edge asking questions and Bronwen answering them.

Finally she said gently, "Mark, God is going to reveal His purposes for you in due time."

But Edge was a man who wanted direct answers to direct questions. And he wanted those answers now. Almost angrily, he snapped, "Well, it seems to me that if God is so powerful, He could make His business better understood!"

He set down the bottle again and clasped his hands together, squeezing them as hard as he could. "I was in a church once, and I heard a preacher say, 'God helps those that help themselves.'" He looked up at Bronwen, his lips pressed tightly together in the spirit of determination. "I guess that's been my religion. I've been helping myself ever since."

"I don't know who that preacher was, but he didn't get that out of the Bible. The Bible *never* says God helps those that help themselves. It says that God helps those who *can't* help themselves. That's what the story of Jesus dying on the cross is about, Mark. He died because we couldn't help ourselves. But since He has

died, we can all find God. I hope you can believe that."
She leaned toward him and put her hand over his.

Mark Edge felt a strange emotion going through him, and as he looked into his navigator's eyes he knew he had rarely, if ever, seen such compassion and love in a human being.

"Even if you never lifted a finger for yourself or anyone else, God would still love you. Jesus would have died for you all the same."

Bronwen now was looking toward one of the *Daystar*'s open portals. He followed her gaze outside into the open heavens and thought, *How strange it is that certain people come into our lives. I wouldn't admit this to Bronwen, but somehow I know that Bronwen Llewellen is on this ship for some purpose that has to do with me. I can't fool myself any longer. It's no accident that she's here.*

"Petroski to Llewellen!"

"Yes, what is it, Chief?" Bronwen spoke up.

"I need you down here to check the navigation console while I check the reroutes."

"Why did you have to perform reroutes on the navigation system? It was working perfectly."

"Heck was fiddling around with the circuits to the shields. He accidentally shorted out one of the navigational subsystems."

"And now we have to reroute circuits that were damaged." If Bronwen had a bare nerve, Heck was the one who usually stepped on it.

Petroski said. "Heck has already fixed most of the damage. I never saw anybody repair burned circuits so quick. I think he's had a lot of practice. Anyway, we just need to check his work to be sure."

Bronwen shook her head back and forth as she laughed. "I have to go, Captain." She stood up, and as he rose she examined him with her calm dark blue eyes. "God isn't far from you, Mark."

"It feels like He's a million miles away."

"That's where you're mistaken. He's not only out there among those stars. He's right here."

Mark Edge stood watching as the door slid open and Bronwen disappeared. As it closed, he muttered aloud, "I've got a shipload of Christians, and I still can't figure it out. What in the world am I missing?"

7

Sir Richard's Plan

Ringo entered the busy crew lounge and took a quick look about. He had always liked the lounge better than any other spot on the spacecraft, and now once again he was impressed by what he saw.

"How's it going, Ringo?" asked a voice from a nearby table. The grunt Myron was sipping a drink.

"OK, I guess. What are you drinking?" Ringo asked as he joined him.

Myron was a "grunt" because it was his job to do most of the physical labor aboard ship. He was just five feet eight inches tall but was strong as an ox. Ringo was exactly one inch taller than Myron, but the grunt was twenty-one and Ringo was fourteen.

"You're too young to be drinking something this strong. Why, if you was to sip just the slightest amount, you'd pass out." Myron's eyes sparkled.

"So what is it—some sort of rum drink native to Bellinka Two?"

"What's Bellinka Two?"

"That's Ivan Petroski's home planet."

Myron gulped down half the dark brown liquid in his glass. "Shows you how much I know!"

Ringo tried to be patient but was having a difficult time. Myron wanted to horse around. Ringo had other things on his mind. "What *is* the stuff?" he asked impatiently.

"It's called soda."

"Soda? That doesn't sound like it's from Bellinka Two."

"Soda is actually from here on Earth. It's very rare and can only be found in the nicer health food stores now."

"So it's a health drink?"

"I guess so. The history books I studied said that people used to drink soda whenever there was something wrong with the drinking water. They used to carry it around with them everywhere. They never knew when they might run into some germ-infested water supply, so they drank soda rather than become sick. As far as anyone knows, nothing alive can exist in soda. In fact, back in the twentieth century they used this stuff to clean the corrosion off the ancient batteries of that time."

Ringo didn't know if he was ready to tackle soda yet. "Maybe I'll try some later." He looked away, wondering, *Who in his right mind would want to drink that stuff? It doesn't sound like a health drink to me!*

Myron held up his glass to the light and watched the thousands of soda bubbles dance through the caramel-colored liquid. Then he downed the rest of the drink in one huge gulp. It was obvious he could easily become hooked on whatever it was.

Ringo was still looking out the large portal windows that formed the outside wall of the crew lounge. New Houston Spaceport was the cream of the crop. The views from a ship on the space dock extended hundreds of miles in any direction. To the east, he could just make out the Gulf of Mexico.

Down below he could see Studs and Dai maneuvering a large container around the cargo area. Studs was sopping wet with perspiration. Dai Bando appeared not to have a drop on him.

Ringo turned back to Myron. "Has Simms had any more trouble since his accident on the Merlina trip?"

"He's doing great. Dr. Cole did a good job of fixing him."

"Well, I'll see you later. I see someone I want to talk to."

Having noticed Lt. Tara Jaleel seated in front of a large bay, Ringo edged closer. He could not help being nervous, for he had received too many bruises at the hands of the weapons officer during her martial arts sessions to be otherwise.

Actually he was fascinated by the woman and re-pelled at the same time. She was a descendant of the Masai tribe, which had originated in Africa. They were the continent's fiercest tribe—no other warriors had been able to stand against them—and this fierceness had come down to Jaleel. The tall woman loved battle of any kind.

"Uh—excuse me, Lieutenant Jaleel—"

Turning her head, Jaleel studied Ringo with some-thing like contempt. "What do you want, Smith?"

"Well . . . actually I would like to ask you a ques-tion. If you don't mind, that is."

Giving the young Ranger an icy look, Jaleel shrugged her shoulders and, without speaking, motioned toward a chair.

Quickly Ringo pulled up the chair, cleared his throat, and began the speech that he had prepared.

"Lieutenant Jaleel, I haven't forgotten the things you told me about Shiva."

Interest brightened the dark eyes of the weapons officer. Ringo knew she was excited about only two things in this world—battle and her goddess, Shiva. "I'm glad to hear that you have a little judgment, Ringo

Smith. Do you still have the image that you bought on Morlandria?"

"Yes, I do." Ringo reached into his pocket and pulled out a small bronze statue.

Fitting snugly in the palm of his hand, it looked like a woman who was frozen in a dance. Framed by a circle of bronze from the waist up, she had six arms, which were extended and holding onto the bronze circle equal distances around its circumference.

The detail and engravings were masterfully done, and Ringo believed the small figure was far more valuable than the price he had paid for it. He imagined the statue shivered in his hand as he brought it out into the light.

"The man I bought it from," he said, "seemed reluctant to talk about Shiva."

"He was wise," Jaleel murmured. She reached out her hand and, when Ringo placed the image in her palm, held it reverently. Something like a smile turned the corners of her lips upward. It was impossible to guess what was going on in her mind, for her face was like a mask. Only Jaleel's eyes ever revealed the emotions that went on inside her. Usually these were anger or dissatisfaction. Handing it back, she said, "What is your question?"

Ringo placed the image carefully back in his pocket. He hesitated, then asked what had been on his mind for some time. "Lieutenant, is Shiva responsible for your courage? I mean, everybody knows you're the bravest member of the crew, being the weapons officer and all, and I was just wondering how you got to be that way."

For just a moment, suspicion glinted in Tara Jaleel's eyes. But then, apparently seeing that his question was innocent enough, she relaxed somewhat.

"Your question is complex, Ranger," she said quietly, and, leaning back, she began talking about her past.

It was a simple history. She had known nothing but being trained for battle since early childhood. Her girlhood had been spent learning various kinds of weaponry, military history of the cosmos, and the martial arts in all forms.

Jaleel had found herself especially drawn to the martial art called Jai-Kando. This particular martial art originated with the sixth-century Indian Hindu religion. The name was from the Eastern belief of "Jain Jayati," which meant "the believer who conquers." When Tara became of age, she had entered the Space Academy, completed all the courses of study, and graduated at the top of her class.

Then she said in what was little more than a whisper, "When I first began, I had some fear. When I went into battle, I held back for fear of being maimed or killed." She went on for some time describing her early days, and then her voice became stronger. She leaned forward and, without appearing to notice, seized Ringo by the arm. Her grip was like iron and actually hurt, but seemingly she was unaware of it.

"But then something came into my life that made me altogether different."

"Was it . . . Shiva?"

"Yes!" Her grip tightened, and the officer spoke with a fierce joy. "When I started to follow Shiva—I can only describe it in an image that you might understand. It was like I was in darkness, but when I gave myself over to Shiva, it was as if a light came on in my head. She made me realize how weak I was, and she promised to make me strong—stronger than any other warrior." A shiver went over the big woman, and her lips curled upward in a smile again. "And she has kept her promise. She has made me a warrior so that I can fulfill her will."

Ringo listened spellbound as for some time the weapons officer went on, telling him how her goddess had changed her.

At last Jaleel looked at him and said, "So. That is why I follow Shiva. Because I want to be strong."

"Everyone wants to be strong," Ringo said thoughtfully.

"In that, young man, you are correct. Strength is the secret of the universe. Not love, as your Christian God would say. Love is weak and foolish," she said. "Strength is the answer that we all seek for."

Ringo, however, was troubled by two things.

First, he felt guilty over possessing the idol of Shiva that he had bought. All three girls—Raina, Mei-Lani, and Jerusha—had warned him not to traffic in such things. He had gone against their advice, and somehow a tiny alarm bell had been ringing in his mind ever since.

Then, it bothered him that by coming to Tara Jaleel he was again turning aside from the advice of all of his friends among the Rangers.

Ringo had told the truth about strength. He had been brought up in an orphanage, and the experience had marked him. He had been one of the smallest boys there, and he had been tormented by bullies and by a pair of cruel administrators. Finally he had reached the Academy, hoping it would be different, but there too he had been unsuccessful. Now among the Space Rangers, he still felt inferior—even to Heck Jordan. Ringo longed to be strong, and he had noted that the weapons officer, whatever her faults, was totally fearless and forceful.

He knew he would be ashamed if his friends

learned he had come to Jaleel, but still he had to do something!

"I've tried to be strong, but it hasn't worked," he said honestly. "I'm the weakest one on the whole crew." He looked up, saying, "Is there any way I can be strong and courageous like you are, Lieutenant?"

"Why do you want this strength?" Jaleel demanded.

"Well, to be truthful, I like Raina St. Clair very much, and if I were strong, like maybe Dai Bando, I think she would notice me."

Jaleel laughed cynically. "Shiva's not interested in your love affairs! She is seeking people to worship her. You're going to have to make a choice, Ringo Smith. Either the weak Christian God, who died futilely on a cross, or the all-powerful Shiva."

Ringo kept on looking at the weapons officer, as fear and confusion swept through him. He felt drawn both ways—longing for strength and courage, where he had known nothing but weakness and fear all of his life, and at the same time sensing unspoken dread of what he would be committing himself to if he followed Tara Jaleel's goddess.

Finally he whispered, "I've only wanted two things in my whole life. One is to find my father—if he's still alive—and the other is to have a friend like Raina."

Jaleel listened. Then she lowered her head, and Ringo could not see her eyes. She seemed to be thinking.

Lifting her eyes, she said, "Listen to me, Ringo Smith. I can understand what you're going through. You want to be strong—so did I. And you want companionship. Well, I long for that, too, despite all the hardness you see in me."

"You do?"

"Certainly! And it will come to me—as it will come to you, Ringo."

67

"Do you really think so?"

"To Shiva all things are possible." She went on, talking earnestly of the glories of Shiva.

Ringo listened. Her words sank into him, taking root in his mind, and he shoved aside all that he knew was right as he listened to Tara Jaleel speak.

Thousands of years ago, the Irons family had emigrated to a planet-sized moon that circled the giant planet Olmec. Olmec was one of a dozen gaseous giants that orbited the star Algol in the Pegasus Constellation. Richard Irons's ancestors had named their new home Palenque because of the Mayan-style pyramids that dotted the moon's entire surface. These were massive structures built by early colonists and with miles of underground tunnels that latticed the earth hundreds of feet deep. These tunnels linked the network of pyramids together.

Richard Irons was born in the chief pyramid on Palenque. Twice the height of any of the other pyramids, it clearly stood out as the dwelling place of the lord of Palenque, his father, Sir Ringo Irons.

When Richard Irons decided to build his own headquarters, he did not think small. Most men have to consider expense when designing their homes and their places of business, but not so with Sir Richard. He put up a structure that was like nothing else in the cosmos. Sir Richard Irons constructed a glass and titanium pyramid three times the size of his father's pyramid, which it overlooked.

From the top of his new business headquarters, Irons was able to look down on his dead father's home with a heart of bitterness. The ancient pyramid, with the symbol of an eagle affixed to the top, stood as a reminder to Richard of what he had been denied.

Irons stood looking out of his window at his family's royal pyramid, standing at his feet, and he laughed mockingly. "Well, Father, you may have cheated me out of what's mine, but I beat you. I still rule over your people in spite of you."

This room formed the apex of Sir Richard's glass and titanium pyramid. From here, he could see in any direction for hundreds of miles. Every security device known to science was incorporated in his private castle. He could look out, but no one could look in. The building was also replete with hidden tunnels throughout. Some were known only to Irons and to his second in command, Francesca Del Ray.

Sir Richard turned then, walked across the room, and sat at an ornate table made of solid gold. For a time he sipped his drink and looked across the table at Francesca, his eyes approving of her.

Indeed, Francesca Del Ray was stunning. Her blonde hair was long, her blue eyes were electric, and she wore a gold lamé gown. She was attentive to him as always. She was, in fact, the female equivalent of Irons, ruthless as a fallen angel. Her pride and ambition knew no bounds. The only thing that motivated her was power. Power to control others and make them yield to her will by force. Power to crush. Power to destroy.

"As soon as my plans are successful, my dear," Irons said, his voice smooth yet strong and powerful, "I will rule the whole quadrant—except for the Cygnus Sector."

"That has been a troublesome area, hasn't it, Richard?"

"That will not always be the case."

"I trust not, and I look forward to the day when we will rule the whole cosmos."

Suddenly a signal chimed.

"Blast!" Irons muttered with irritation. He pressed the door button near his chair. "What is it?" he demanded.

A tall aide wearing a distinctive crimson uniform appeared and announced, "Sir, the *Jackray* is approaching the P54."

"Good!" Irons snapped. "Tell the commander they are to place Zaria and the two cadets into the *Jackray*'s brig!"

"Yes sir!"

As the aide started to leave, Irons called after him, "By the way, have the P54 destroyed before the *Jackray* heads back to port."

"It shall be done, sir."

"Wait!" Francesca exclaimed. She turned to Irons and said, "Would it not be a valuable prize, that P54? Could it not be towed back to headquarters?"

He shook his head. "You don't understand, my dear. That P54 would be tracked. You may rest assured that Commandant Lee will never give up trying to find it! It has to be destroyed!"

"I suppose so, but it's a shame to lose such a valuable ship."

"It doesn't really matter. It's possible the Denebians will destroy it before we can get there, anyway." He turned back to the aide. "On your way! See that my orders are carried out!"

As soon as the man left and the door automatically closed, Irons began laughing softly.

Staring at his face, Del Ray said, "I can't see anything amusing about the situation."

"Can't you, my dear? You remember Zaria, do you not?"

"That witch!" Francesca Del Ray was intensely jealous of any attractive woman. "She's nothing but a charlatan!"

70

"No, she's more than that, my dear," Irons said more seriously. "She has powers that could be used. But she's stubborn. We will have to get rid of her."

"Then why are you smiling?"

"I'm thinking that she will be angry as a Tasminthian hornet because I intend to have her thrown into the brig! I would love to see her face when she realizes I don't choose to be a part of her plans!"

"So would I," Del Ray said. "So would I. And perhaps we shall see it. Perhaps we will see even more than that."

8

Into Harm's Way

Just as Jerusha Ericson and Raina St. Clair came onto the bridge, Capt. Mark Edge looked up from the helm computer. Irritation was etched on his face. "Hey, you two!" he yelled. "Come over here!"

"What's wrong with *him?*" Raina whispered.

"I don't know," Jerusha whispered back, "but he's mad. You can always tell, can't you?"

The two girls took their station across from the captain, who glared at them. "Have you seen Heck?"

"Why, no, we just returned to the ship, Captain. Have you lost him?" Jerusha said, a smile pulling at the corners of her lips. The atmosphere aboard the *Daystar* was generally nonmilitary and highly relaxed. She knew that Edge hated to be teased, but she felt free to do it deliberately sometimes, as now.

Jerusha apparently succeeded in irritating the captain. Drawing back his datacorder, he sent it sailing across the bridge. It crashed into the bulkhead, disintegrated, and fell to the floor in pieces.

"Well," Jerusha said, "I guess you showed that datacorder a thing or two."

"Ranger Ericson, be quiet!"

"Aye, sir. I won't say another word about your behaving like a child."

"I am not behaving like a child!"

"No, of course not. Space fleet captains always throw their equipment against the wall and break it to pieces."

Edge glowered at her, daring her to say one more word. She did not.

But Raina did. "Really, Captain," she said quietly, "throwing things around will never solve anything."

"And you keep your mouth zipped, too, Ranger St. Clair!" Edge said crossly. He whirled and walked toward the navigational console, his back stiff.

Knowing her captain well, Jerusha dared to say, "It's funny, isn't it, Raina, how a grown, mature man can act like a little boy and throw fits."

"That's exactly what he reminds me of," Raina replied. "A little boy who's had his feelings hurt." She began to giggle, and Jerusha joined her.

The girls intended him to hear, and he did. He spun around from the navigational console and stomped across the bridge to tower over them. "Let's have some discipline on this ship. And knock off that giggling," he said. "You sound like a girls' school!"

"Have you ever been in a girls' school, Captain Edge?" Jerusha asked innocently. Laughter was still in her dark blue eyes.

"I've been in a lot of them! They're all filled with silly girls who only think about silly things! Now, where have you two been, and why did you leave the ship when there's so much work left to do?"

At one time Jerusha Ericson might have been intimidated by the exasperated look on the captain's face, but several difficult and dangerous missions had taught her to know him. He could, indeed, be hard occasionally, but she had learned that underneath was a layer of gentleness—the mention or even the suspicion of which made him furious. Now she thought, *He still looks like a little boy. All he has to do is stick his lip out, and he would be exactly like one.*

Aloud she said, "We went for a visit to the Academy, Captain."

His expression changed to one of puzzlement. "Why in the world would you want to go there?" he demanded. "It seems to me that's the last place any of you Rangers would want to go. If Inch found you there, she would toss you out on your heads!"

Jerusha knew that the description was very accurate. She began speaking quickly. "I've been worried about Karl Bentlow, sir."

"Karl Bentlow? And why would you be worried about *him?*"

"Because it's been weeks since we landed at New Houston Spaceport, and I haven't heard anything from him."

"Why should you hear from him?" Edge said. "Bentlow and Von Kemp—those two are a pair of spoiled brats. I wouldn't trust either of them with a tricycle much less a corvette! I always thought things were going to pot at the Space Academy, and now I know it!"

"You may be right about that, Captain," Jerusha broke in, "but I've been worried all the same."

"Worried about those two?" he said, still puzzled.

"She's not worried about Olga," Raina explained. "Just about Karl."

"Oh ho, you're worried about Karl!" A note of triumph edged the voice of the captain, and he grinned broadly. "So the high and mighty Ensign Jerusha Ericson, engineering genius, has fallen for that pretty boy!"

"I have not fallen for anybody!" Jerusha said coldly and clearly, biting out the words. "But I did see another side to Karl on this last mission. I think he's changing, and we became friends."

"Friends? I'll say they became friends." Raina was a kindly girl, but she simply could not refrain from poking fun at Jerusha's romances. "She hasn't thought of anything except Karl's 'friendship' since we docked at New Houston Spaceport," she teased.

"Raina, stop it!" Jerusha snapped, flushing. She turned back to the captain and saw that he was still grinning broadly at her. "And I wish you'd take that grin off your face!"

"I'm sorry. I didn't mean to insult you," Edge said rather loudly. "I wouldn't want to interfere with the love life of one of my genius Space Rangers."

Jerusha flushed even more rosily. "Captain," she said, hoping to change the subject, "I did something you may not approve of."

"*Something* I may not approve of?" he barked. "You've done *everything* I don't approve of!"

"But this is something even more serious than the other things."

"What have you done this time, Jerusha?" Edge asked uneasily, watching her face.

"Well, to tell the truth, I talked Ringo into hacking into the Academy computer banks."

Edge turned pale. He groped behind him for his chair, fell into it, and then put his face into his hands and shook his head. "She—talked—Ringo—into— hacking—into—the—Academy's—computer—banks. I—can't—believe—what—I'm—hearing!" He looked up, an agonized expression on his face. "Jerusha Ericson, do you have the slightest idea how much trouble you may have caused all of us?"

"It'll be all right, Captain," Jerusha said hurriedly. "I had to do it!"

"She had to do it," Edge echoed. "Well, what did you find out, if I may be so bold as to ask?"

"Ringo found out that the P54 combat corvette that

Karl and Olga were flying has never returned to the spaceport."

"That doesn't mean anything." Edge shrugged. "Maybe they were ordered somewhere else."

"We thought of that, but Ringo was absolutely certain that there had not been any new orders issued to them. There would have been a record of it on the spaceport database."

"Are you certain about all of this, Jerusha, or is it just something you and Ringo dreamed up?"

"You can check with Ringo, sir, but it's all true. All they knew at the Academy was that the P54 was due back weeks ago, and it hasn't returned."

Raina broke in then, saying, "That's why we went to the Academy, Captain. We had to find out if Karl and Olga had gotten back some other way."

"I suppose you announced to everybody that you were there to search the secret records of the Space Academy?" Edge said. He stood to his feet and scowled at them. "I suppose you didn't bother to keep any of this a secret?"

"All we did was check at the registrar's office," Raina said, "but no one would talk to us."

"No, the Academy staff were very closed. They wouldn't say anything about Karl and Olga," Jerusha added. "But they acted like there was nothing wrong."

"That's when Jerusha demanded to talk to someone in charge."

"Oh, that's wonderful! That's just wonderful! I suppose you went right to Commander Inch?"

"Why, yes, that's what I did," Jerusha said.

"So now you have alerted the Commander of the Intergalactic Space Academy that we are able to break into their databases!"

"Why, certainly not, Captain!" Raina said, indignation tinging her voice. "All I asked was that we be allowed to speak to Karl or Olga."

"And what did Commander Inch say?"

"She took one look at us and had us thrown out," Raina admitted. "When we protested, they threw us out bodily." She rubbed her right hip. "I landed on the same spot where they threw me out the first time."

"I can't believe what you two have done! You have violated every basic procedure of the Intergalactic Council, the Girl Scouts, and everything else!"

"Please, Captain," Jerusha begged, "don't be angry."

"Why shouldn't I be angry?"

"Because I've—well, I've sensed, ever since we left Morlandria almost, that something is dreadfully wrong with Karl and Olga."

Captain Edge's eyes narrowed thoughtfully.

Jerusha knew he often got exasperated with her, but she also suspected he had learned to respect that "sense of things" she sometimes had.

"What do you mean? You feel they're in trouble?"

"Yes, sir, I do," Jerusha said. "All the time I kept telling myself it was just a silly feeling, but now—from the way they acted at the Space Academy—I *know* something's wrong."

When Capt. Mark Edge made up his mind, he could move as quickly as a striking snake. "Go clean up," he told them, "and send Heck to me as soon as possible."

As Jerusha turned to follow Raina away from the bridge, the captain yelled after her, "And *never* hack into the Academy computers again! Do you hear me, Ranger Ericson?"

Jerusha turned back and whispered, "Aye, sir. I will obey orders."

She left him staring after her, shaking his head, and muttering, "That'll be the day!"

Aboard the Magnum Deep Space Cruiser that was the flagship of Intergalactic Command, Chief Executive Officer Matt Moyer chimed the door of the ship's captain.

"Enter," Pursey responded quietly.

As the door iris swirled open, Major Moyer saw his best friend bent over his datacorder. He entered and crossed the aqua-colored carpet toward him.

Looking up, Pursey nodded toward a chair and smiled. "What's up, Matt? I've been expecting you." It was a greeting that Pursey had called out to Moyer for more than twenty years.

Major Moyer sat down in one of three chairs that were located in front of Pursey's desk. It was a large desk made of genuine Earthborn black oak. The grain was rich and dark. Pursey always said he preferred the feel of real wood over the many synthetics that had been invented over the last thousand years. The cushions on the chairs were covered with Dernof leather dyed scarlet. The ox skin of the planet Dernof was the softest and hardiest furniture upholstery material in the galaxy.

The only other pieces of furniture in the captain's office were a large couch, covered in the same red material, and a coffee table in front of the couch. It was made of the same black oak. The office was businesslike but comfortable.

Moyer scratched the left side of his head with his right hand. It was a behavior pattern that his friend would know well. He was worried.

"Nathan, the *Cromwell* will be reaching the P54 shortly, and to tell you the truth—" Moyer looked straight into Pursey's dark hazel eyes "—I'm very concerned about the Denebians. You know how they are. They shoot first and don't ask questions at all. We've already lost several ships in their space. Frankly, I would hate to be within two sectors of Cygnus myself!"

"If it helps you any, Matt, your concern is shared by Commandant Lee and myself. We don't want to instigate an incident with them. Especially one that could cause an interstellar war."

Pursey looked over at the strategic star map that hung on the wall to his right. "We've kept peace with them just by staying out of their space. We've made them mad enough by imposing space beacons next to their space boundaries. For some reason, they haven't destroyed them yet!"

Moyer said as he leaned forward in his chair, "This mission has everybody at headquarters walking on pins and needles—including me!"

"We understand that, Matt. The truth is that the P54 and the crew aboard her are our responsibility. We're praying for the best but preparing for the worst. Not to mention the obvious—it would be a disaster to lose two knowledgeable cadets and our latest scientific secrets to the Denebians."

Pursey stood up and walked toward the star map. "I've just been working on a plan that maybe will distract the Denebians while the *Cromwell* attempts the rescue mission." He adjusted a few controls, and the Cygnus Sector appeared on the screen. "I want you to position six of our Magnum Deep Space Cruisers in these areas." He indicated each position with his laser pointer. "Send them to their stations one at a time. By the time the *Cromwell* reaches the P54, they must be in place. Let me know the moment they reach their positions."

Moyer saw that the positions indicated by Pursey were three sectors away from the P54. "What if they attack?" he asked in a serious voice. "The Magnums will be too far away to help."

"Then we'll have to do what we have to do. We're going into harm's way. Hopefully, we can get out of there before anything happens."

Pursey's forehead creased in deep thought. "I know the Denebians will think twice before attacking six of our most powerful ships. They respect our strength. We'll use the Magnums to draw away their attention from the P54."

"What are the Magnums going to do when they get there?"

"If I've figured correctly, all they have to do is show up. Before the Denebians can figure out what to do, the *Cromwell* will rescue the P54, and the Magnums will disappear as quickly as they arrived." Pursey walked over to Moyer and put a hand on his friend's shoulder.

Moyer looked up at him and said, "Well, I guess that's why they pay you the big money."

9

The Medallion

Open your mouth—wider!"
Heck Jordan, his shirt off, was sitting on a table
in the sick bay. "If I open it any wider, I'll swallow
myself," he complained. Then he made an enormous
cavern of his mouth and stared almost pop-eyed at Dr.
Temple Cole.

Cole looked down Heck's throat and made a nota-
tion on the small notebook in her hand.

"Well, was everything all right in there?" Heck
asked. He looked unhealthy, for his stomach flopped
over his belt and his face was rounder than it should
have been.

As Temple Cole looked up from her notebook, she
observed, "You know, Ranger Jordan, if you'd lose some
weight, you'd really be a fine-looking young man."

"I'm already a fine-looking young man!"

"You look unhealthy! I've often wondered," the
doctor mused, "why it is that people who would be
very attractive if they were more slender don't lose
weight."

"I look just fine. Don't worry about my looks," Heck
said. "What about all these bruises that Tara Jaleel put
on me?"

"In just a moment. Heck, you're five ten, and you
weigh two hundred thirty pounds, and most of it is
blubber."

"I prefer to call it excess flesh."

"You can call it anything you want to. You're overweight, and you need to lose it. It's not helping you a bit. As young as you are, you've got plenty of time to do something about it. And as I said, you'd look better. More trim."

"I think I've got gland trouble."

"You don't have gland trouble." Reaching over to Heck's tunic pocket, the doctor pulled forth several candy bars. "You have candy bar trouble. Food trouble, to put it more bluntly! You eat more than you need. You eat all the time!"

"I do not!"

"When are you not eating?"

"When I'm asleep." Heck grinned. "I've given up eating candy bars when I'm asleep."

Temple Cole shook her head in despair. "I can't get any sense out of you. Every time I try to talk seriously, you try to be funny." She looked at him more closely and said, "I think it's just an act you put on, Heck."

"What is?" he asked innocently.

"You put on this arrogant, know-it-all act because you're really not sure of yourself."

"Oh, I didn't know you were a psychologist, Doc. Well, it's all my mother's fault. She wouldn't let me have my cereal when I was six weeks old. It's all her fault, Doc. I can't help myself. I'm just a victim."

"Oh, shut up!"

"Shut up? Is that any kind of professional dialogue? What do you mean, shut up? Is that what they taught you at medical school?"

Temple Cole gazed at the boy and could not keep back a smile. "I can't do anything to help you until you're ready to help yourself, Heck."

"Well, you can help me with these bruises. That's why I came in here, anyway. To get some kind of ease for my bones. Lieutenant Jaleel must have broken something when she threw me against the wall."

"That's just training. We all go through it."

"Not like this. She was mean, Doc, real mean!"

Dr. Cole spent a few moments going over Heck and finally admitted, "You do have some pretty bad bruises there. I'd better look you over for internal injuries." She ran several checks, then asked, "Whatever did you do that made the lieutenant throw you against the wall?"

"I don't have any idea. It wasn't my fault. *Yow!* That hurts!" he complained. "One second I was talking to Ringo, and the next second I was flying through the air, and I crashed into the wall."

"Did the lieutenant say anything?"

"No, but you should have seen her face. I think she was just mad because she couldn't get the best of Dai Bando. That always makes her mad, you know."

"Does it?"

"Oh, sure! She can beat up on anybody else, but she's never once laid a hand on Dai. It really eats her lunch, Doc. The rest of us all get a kick out of it."

"Well, then, you probably laughed at her, and no one likes to be laughed at."

"Well, excuse me! I laugh at her, and she breaks my bones! What's fair about that?"

"Was that all there was to it?"

"It certainly was not!" Heck declared indignantly. "Then that monster of a dog that belongs to Jerusha jumped on me and took my candy bar away from me!"

The doctor smiled. "I suppose that hurt you worse than getting slammed against the wall. Well, stay away from Jaleel for a while."

Eagerly Heck said, "I think you should give me a notice that I'm to avoid martial arts. Yes, I think that would be best, don't you, Doctor?"

"Well, perhaps for a few days."

Heck chortled happily while she filled out a slip of paper. But when she handed him a second one, he gaped at it. "This says no sweets for a week!"

"That's right. And that's our bargain. I'll get you out of martial arts, and you stop eating food that's bad for you. Both for one week."

"But I'm hungry right now. Don't you have a piece of candy or something around here? I think I'm growing faint."

Dr. Cole rolled her eyes while shaking her head in an expression of futility. "Heck, quit wasting my breath. Now, get out of my office!"

At that moment Ringo walked into the sick bay. He looked anxiously toward Heck and asked the doctor, "Is he OK? Any bones broken?"

"No, just bruises—and those mostly to his pride." She looked at the two young Rangers and smiled. "I've got to step outside for a moment. You wait here, Ringo. And, Heck, I'm not through with you yet."

"What did she say to you, Heck?" Ringo asked when the doctor was gone.

"Why, she's no more a doctor than I am. You know what her cure-all is? 'Stop eating candy.' Why, that wouldn't help me!"

Looking down at Heck's middle, Ringo said, "It might. You're really overdoing the candy, Heck. You ought to cut back a *little* bit."

"Now, don't you start on me. I've had about enough of this persecution of—what shall I call it?—*mature* people."

"You mean fat people."

"That's not politically correct! Stop calling me that!"

Ringo jumped up and sat on the hard table beside Heck. As he did so, the medallion that he always wore fell free from his tunic.

Heck reached for it, anxious to turn the conversation away from his appetite. "You always wear this thing, don't you?"

"It's about all I got of my past, Heck."

"Where did you get it?"

As Ringo fingered the medallion, Heck could see a large bird on the front side and then the likeness of a man on the back side. There was also unusual writing on the medallion that Heck didn't recognize.

Ringo flipped the medallion back under his shirt. "All I can tell you is that my mother left it for me when she died. I was a baby at the time, so I don't have any memories of her. Later on, the staff at the state orphanage gave me the medallion and a letter. The letter explained that the medallion had belonged to my grandfather and I was not to lose it."

"Well, I can sympathize with you about state orphanages. I didn't have much of a good childhood myself."

"If you didn't grow up in the place I did, you don't know anything about hard times." Ringo looked at the floor and drew his lips into a fine line. His brown hair hung down, covering his forehead.

Heck thought for once about someone other than himself, and he asked, "Why was it so bad? What happened?"

"That orphanage was run just like a prison. You never knew if your new bunkmate was just another orphan or if he was a convicted murderer. Most of the time I found out very quickly and learned to do what I needed to survive."

Heck's curiosity was getting the best of him. "Like what?" The candy man found himself wanting details.

"Heck, I don't really like to talk about it. But— well, I had to do some dishonest things sometimes. Many times all I had was the choice between two evils.

Like, should I steal a set of keys or get my head beat in?" Ringo looked toward the door. Then he tapped his finger nervously against the table he was sitting on. "I'll tell you one thing, though."

Heck decided to be silent.

"There are worse things than getting a head beating," Ringo told him. "Maybe I'll talk to you about it some other time."

Heck had to admire his friend. Ringo had suffered in silence for the most part. Suffering on any level was too much for Heck.

"OK. I'm here whenever you need me." Heck glanced down at his shirt pocket, then stuck his finger in it, hoping to find a candy bar. Not finding one, he frowned. But then he turned back to Ringo. "You still having problems with the nightmare?"

Ringo sighed. Then he said very seriously, "Yes, I still have it."

"Tell me about it again. Maybe I can figure out what it means."

Ringo started again the story that he had told many times before. He claimed no one had ever been able to explain it to him.

"They sent me to the planet Terraa to fix some quirky computer problems they were having. You know that. Everything was going great, so one night I decided to take a hike toward a nearby mountain. I needed a break, and I thought the exercise would help me concentrate." Ringo started tapping faster on the tabletop. "Nobody had told me yet about the two full moons." He grimaced.

"*Two* full moons."

"I found out that once every sixty days, both moons that circle Terraa are full at the same time. They're very beautiful, and they light up the planet like day. Anyway, taking a hike in the moonlight seemed like it would be fun. So I started off."

"What's so bad about that?"

"I'm not finished—as you know. Nobody had told me about the Daqtils, either. When the two moons are full—every sixty days—these batlike things fly out of their nesting caves. I guess something about the two moons draws them out. They have leathery wings and faces full of razor-sharp teeth. They're carnivorous, and they're very hungry."

Ringo looked at his rotund friend and managed a small smile. "Heck, you must know how that feels."

"Very funny," Heck responded sarcastically. "If I didn't eat for sixty days, I don't think I'd be alive!"

"I'm sorry, Heck, but you really *do* need to lose some weight."

"Get off the weight thing. I've had enough sermons today. Go on with the story."

Ringo continued recounting his experience. "I was walking across a large field when suddenly the Daqtils were flying everywhere. I didn't know what they were, and the moonlight really made them look eerie. They started diving at me like starfighters. Before I knew it, they'd knocked me to the ground. I couldn't move. I couldn't even yell. Something kept me from making a sound. I found out later that the first Daqtils to fly into me had injected me with a paralyzing poison.

"When I was helpless on the ground, it looked like a thousand of the creatures landed right on top of me. Several of them started to bite me. I tried to scream, move my arms, get up and run, anything, but nothing worked. All I could do was lie there and let these flying meat eaters start to make a meal out of me."

Though Heck had heard the story before, he felt the hair on the back of his neck standing straight up.

"Then—all of a sudden—for some reason I don't understand, the Daqtils started screeching and flying off of me. As fast as they could, they headed back toward the mountain."

"Something must have scared them off," Heck said simply.

"All I can say is that I should be dead. I was seriously injured and poisoned. I was sort of in and out of consciousness. Then somebody found me. I saw this man leaning over me and telling me not to be afraid. When I finally came to, I was in the medical clinic. I never did meet the man."

"He was the one who scared off the Daqtils," Heck said confidently. "He also took you to the clinic. You were very lucky!"

"I think so, too. Or maybe it wasn't luck. Maybe it was God."

"But you still have nightmares about it," Heck said.

"Yeah. And the nightmare is strange in a couple of ways. First, the Daqtils are not after *me*—they're after the medallion. And second—in the dream, the man doesn't show up. In the dream, I'm all alone trying to save my life until I wake up screaming."

Heck couldn't guess what it all meant. He decided to change the unpleasant subject back to Ringo's parents. "So you don't have any idea who your parents really are. Is that right?"

"I know my mother's dead. I don't know who she was or what she died of. They told me at the orphanage that she was young. I've thought about my father over the years—who was he and where would he be? But I've never found out anything. I expect they're both dead. My mother's letter said that this medallion belonged to *his* father. It's the only thing I possess that came from him."

"And that's not much."

"It's a funny thing about this medallion," Ringo said slowly. "There's something real odd about it."

"What's odd about it? You mean the way it looks?"

"No, not so much that. Although I can't understand the words on it and don't know what the symbols mean either—the eagle and the man on the back. The thing is, I've lost it two or three times."

"Lost it? How'd you do that? You wear it all the time."

"I don't know. I just did. But every time, it somehow turned up again. It came back to me."

"You mean you found it. Nothing odd about that." Heck shrugged.

"No, there's more to it than that. It's almost as if—" Here Ringo hesitated and appeared not to know how to put his thoughts. Finally he shook his head in despair and ended by saying, "It's just . . . *there* again. It's like it just comes back to me."

"Never heard of a thing like that."

Ringo looked at his friend. "Well, that's what happened. I've never told anybody else but you, Heck."

"Well, your secret's safe with me. I wish the things I lose would come back—like candy bars! Did I ever tell you about the time I lost my laser blaster on the planet Zingo?"

The floor plan of the *Jackray*'s brig looked similar to a giant clover. One long corridor led into the central core area. Three clover- shaped cell areas led away from the core. Each cell had a Neurotronic security field at the door. These were invisible until touched. Then the whole doorway would light up with waves of hair-tingling light rays.

Olga bent over Karl and bathed his face with a

cold cloth. He had gotten worse since they had been captured by the crew of the *Jackray*. She had begged the officer who had thrown them in the brig for medical care.

The man had simply laughed, saying, "I don't have any instructions from Sir Richard Irons to coddle prisoners."

"But he might die!" she had cried.

"Everybody dies." The officer had laughed again and slammed the door shut.

For hours—days, it seemed to Olga—they had been locked in the prison area of the *Jackray*, seeing only the crew member who had brought them some food.

Karl lay in a deep sleep—a coma, she thought. His face was pale as paper, and his pulse was thin and irregular. She touched his wrist, felt for the pulse, and then looked at Zaria.

The high priestess was sitting in the lotus position on the other side of their small prison room. Her legs were crossed, and on top of them her palms were turned upright. She was chanting something. She appeared to have lost her exceptional powers completely.

"Zaria, you've got to help me with Karl!"

In scarcely more than a whisper, while keeping her eyes shut, Zaria interrupted her chant. "Keep your mouth closed! What can be done is being done."

Olga decided that she would indeed stay quiet. The anger—no, the rage—that had come over Zaria's face terrified her to the core of her being. A chill ran through her, and Olga realized that the temperature of the cell was dropping. It was becoming very, very cold. She huddled close to Karl, trying to keep him warm with her body heat.

I sure hope my message got through, she thought as she closed her eyes and waited.

10

Daystar Is on Her Own

The dining room for once was empty—except for Capt. Mark Edge. Being captain of a starship was something he had always longed for, but at times the responsibilities wearied him. He had just come in after a long, hard night of working on plans for improving the *Daystar*, only to find that he had missed breakfast.

"I wish I were nothing but a pirate again! At least back then I could get some R and R," he muttered.

Manta, the flight cook, suddenly appeared before him.

Manta was a dwarfish man from the planet Skeizar. And he was simply "Manta." The people on Skeizar each had only one name, not two or three names like people from Earth. The crew had learned to put up with Manta's ever present irritability because he was a wonderful cook—much to Heck's delight. Manta and Dr. Cole fought constantly over the menus. Cole believed the food he prepared was far too rich. Manta told her that people need to eat more than rabbit food.

The cook could not stand to have anyone criticize his cooking. He stared in displeasure at the captain's plate. The food was almost untouched.

"What's the matter, Captain? You don't like my cooking?"

"Oh, it's fine, Manta," Mark said quickly, taking a bite of the poached egg and muffin. He liked eggs Benedict, and Manta prepared the dish very well. "I would like to have some more hot coffee, though."

Manta stared at him suspiciously, and the captain defensively took another bite.

Edge played with his eggs until the cook brought him another cup of coffee. He waited until the dwarf left and then leaned back in his chair. His mind was still on the communiqué that he had just received from Commandant Winona Lee. It had been a brief, crisp communication. Closing his eyes, he could see her face and hear her voice:

"The *Cromwell* dropped out of star drive, Captain Edge, and discovered Sir Richard Irons's ship, the *Jackray*, firing on the P54 corvette carrying Karl Bentlow, Olga Von Kemp, and also Zaria, the high priestess of Morlandria. The attack was ineffective, for the shields were up on the corvette.

"Mark, data reveals that the ships were skirting the Cygnus Sector, and even Irons will not be safe there. You know, as well as I, that the Denebians are intolerant of any intrusion into their space. In years past, every ambassadorial ship from Intergalactic Command has been destroyed by the Denebians—"

A sudden noise broke Edge's concentration, and he glanced around to see Contessa padding into the dining room. She promptly sat at his feet, looking up at him expectantly. Her red tongue was lolling out, and her eyes were fixed on him with adoration.

No one, not even Jerusha, who owned the dog, had ever been able to explain her fascination with and unwearied devotion to Capt. Mark Edge. Professedly, he hated dogs. Still, the dog was there, and now her eyes were warm and happy as she gazed up at him and said softly, "*Woof!*"

"*Woof* yourself," Edge muttered. He stared at the beautiful animal, admiring, despite himself, the strength and grace of her perfectly formed body. And he well knew the intelligence that lurked behind those loving brown eyes. "Why do you have to be in love with *me*, Contessa?" he asked plaintively.

"*Woof!*" Contessa said again and pushed forward slightly.

"No, don't knock me down again. You've done that often enough," Mark said. He eyed the animal, then reached out and put melon preserves from Morlandria on a piece of toast. First looking cautiously around the room, he extended it, and Contessa daintily took the morsel from his hand.

She bolted it down, then looked at him again and moaned. "*Woof! Woof!*"

"More, more. Is that what you mean?" He began to layer more toast with the melon preserves and feed it to the large dog, bite by bite. "I don't know why I'm doing this," he grumbled. "All you've ever done for me is cause me grief." He handed her another piece.

And just as he did, a voice came from his left. "Oh, I see you're trying to make up to Contessa."

Whirling around, Mark saw that Jerusha had entered.

A knowing smile was on her face. She came over to his table and sat across from him. "I knew she would win you over in time."

"I just hate this melon jelly. I think it's awful. I was trying to poison her with it," he said, though he suspected that Jerusha Ericson knew her captain better than that.

Her smile widened. "Yes, I've seen how much you hate melon jelly. You eat at least five or six pieces of toast for breakfast every day—literally covered with it."

"Well, I've gotten tired of it," Edge muttered. "Anyway, I don't have time to talk about dogs. I just got a message from Commandant Lee about that corvette we've been talking about."

Instantly Jerusha straightened up. "What did she say, Captain?"

Edge repeated the message. Then he ran his hand over his blond hair in a gesture of despair. "Why in the world would Irons concern himself with a P54 corvette?"

"I can tell you something about that. I had Ringo looking at the P54's computer files."

"The ones you hacked."

"Yes, those," Jerusha said calmly. "Zaria kidnapped Karl and Olga. Then she turned the P54 toward the Cygnus Sector."

"I wonder why."

"Because the Denebians worship Zaria's goddess—Astarte."

"So that's it." Finally he understood. "That's why she headed them toward Cygnus. She knew that the craft wouldn't be destroyed by the Denebians as long as she was on board."

"Yes, but when the *Jackray* arrived, *they* must have taken over the P54."

"That sounds right. We'd better check with the commandant. Come along, Jerusha."

They walked to the bridge—Contessa trailing behind—where Edge sat down in the captain's chair. "Raina, put me through to Commandant Lee."

In a few moments, the commander was on-screen, and Edge was asking, "Commandant Lee, do we know anything new about Bentlow and Von Kemp?"

"Yes, we do! I've just received word from the Magnum Deep Space Cruiser that we sent to intercept the P54." The commandant's face was very serious, and she spoke rapidly. "Before the *Cromwell* could get there, the *Jackray* arrived and boarded the P54. The boarding party found themselves in a fierce battle with Zaria. That blackhearted sorceress somehow was able to kill several of Irons's men. Then the boarding party was reinforced, they had another battle, and they overcame her.

"They put Ensigns Bentlow and Von Kemp, along with Zaria, on board the *Jackray*. When we recovered the P54, we found that while Zaria was busy fighting with Irons's troops, Olga had placed a message in the P54's computer, briefing us on their situation. Von Kemp then programmed the P54 to put full shielding in place as soon as they left the ship."

"That was smart of her. Otherwise, Irons would have destroyed it." The captain knew that Intergalactic Command had technology that was far more advanced than anything Irons possessed.

"Yes, but it looks like Zaria put up quite a fight. Some of the ship's interior doorways were twisted out of shape. Just how, we don't know yet. And, as I've already stated, some of the *Jackray*'s crew lost their lives. But they finally took the woman prisoner."

"So that's where Bentlow and Von Kemp are now—the prisoners of Irons."

"I'm afraid so."

"We've got to do something," Jerusha whispered urgently.

Firing a hard glance at Jerusha, a warning in his eyes, Captain Edge turned back to face the image of Commandant Lee. "What can we do to get them back?"

"Not very much, I'm afraid. Von Kemp's programming to raise the shields saved the ship, but a Magnum Deep Space Cruiser is too large to chance skirting the Cygnus Sector. I had the *Cromwell* leave the area at full speed. The last thing Intergalactic Command needs now is a full-scale war with the Denebians."

"I have an idea where the *Jackray* is headed, sir. Do I have your permission to intercept?"

The commandant was silent a moment. "Captain Edge, you must not start a war. And do *not* enter the Cygnus Sector. The Denebians could easily destroy the *Daystar*." But then she said, "Although, on second thought, since it is a ship unlisted with the Intergalactic Command, they might overlook it. I believe we've provided an adequate decoy placement that might buy you some time . . ."

"Decoys?" asked Edge. "What decoys?"

"We've positioned six Magnum Deep Space Cruisers two sectors away from the P54's last position. We believe the Denebians will give all their attention to the Magnums. As I said, that could buy you some time to get to the *Jackray* and effect a rescue. The Magnums have been ordered to do some fancy maneuvers and then leave. In any event, if the Denebians take even one step toward you, abandon the rescue attempt. Is that understood, Mark?"

"Understood, Commandant."

"Don't underestimate Irons either. You and your crew are not his favorite people. And the *Jackray* could destroy the *Daystar* as easily as the Denebians could." The commander seemed in deep thought for a moment. Then she looked directly at Edge. "I don't want to delve into your past, Mark, but you were once one of Irons's captains."

"That's correct," Edge responded guardedly.

"With your inside information, do you think you could find your way to his headquarters?"

"I could do that with no trouble, Commandant. As a matter of fact, I could land close to his headquarters without being noticed."

A slight smile touched the lips of the commandant. "I see that being a space pirate does have some advantages."

"An *ex*-space pirate, Commandant."

"Of course." Lee smiled more broadly. "Very well. I rather suspected you might come up with something. I'll have the information about the Denebians transferred to the *Daystar* computer. Good hunting, Captain."

The image of Commandant Winona Lee faded, and Edge and the ensign both stood.

Jerusha said, "I told you so! I knew something was wrong two weeks ago!"

Edge stared at her. "It beats me how you know these things."

Jerusha's face turned wistful. "Sometimes I think I'd be happier *not* to sense things sometimes. But for some reason God has blessed me with this gift."

Without thinking, Edge rested a hand on her shoulder. "Well," he said gently, "you seem to use that gift for a good purpose."

Jerusha looked up and smiled faintly. But then she said, "Do you really have a way to get us into Irons's headquarters?"

"Well, I did work for the man at one time. I know his back doors."

"I never have really understood why you left him, Captain."

Edge abruptly removed his hand from Jerusha's shoulder, and an odd look came into his eyes. "I assure you it wasn't all voluntary," he said.

"What was it, Captain? Or can't you tell me?"

For a few seconds Edge was silent, then he said, "For a time I had a . . . well . . . an unusual relationship with Sir Richard's second in command."

"Francesca Del Ray? I've heard about that woman. She's still with Irons, isn't she?"

99

"She is."

Jerusha continued looking up at him. She seemed to want to ask more.

"She was—is—a beautiful woman but one with the morals of a conger eel!"

Jerusha looked at the floor for a moment. Then she raised her head and asked quietly, "Do—did you love her, Captain?"

"No, I didn't love her. Unfortunately, Francesca was attracted to *me*—something that Sir Richard would not tolerate. He got rid of me as though I had the Juno Swine Flu. It was just a bad scene. So now, Jerusha, you understand why Irons really has it in for me. It has to do with a lot more than some stolen technology." He tried to smile. "I hope you never find out *all* about my past."

"I'm learning more about you every day, Captain. Before too much longer, I'll know everything." She smiled back at him. "It's too bad you didn't really get the Juno Swine Flu, though."

"Thanks a lot!"

"I only meant that if you looked like a swine, you wouldn't have the effect on girls that you do."

The two stared at each other in silence.

Then Edge turned to the dog. "Well, Contessa, you still love me, don't you?"

Contessa gazed upward and placed one paw against his knee. *"Woof,"* she said gently, her eyes glowing with love.

At Intergalactic Command headquarters, Commandant Lee, Captain Pursey, and Maj. Matt Moyer were studying one of the fleet's strategic war maps. The chart showed a three-dimensional image of the Cygnus Sector. Off to one side were the six Magnum Deep

Space Cruisers. Two sectors away, the *Daystar* was skirting Denebian space, heading toward the Pegasus Sector—the rumored home of Sir Richard Irons. Nobody in Intergalactic Command knew exactly where his headquarters were.

"Commandant," Moyer said, pointing to the Denebian space closest to the Magnums, "the Denebians have massed twenty-five of their midclass destroyers along this line. The space beacons have picked up another ten Denebian cruisers headed toward the same area. This thing could get hot real quick!" Moyer's voice quaked at the growing urgency of the situation.

"Matt, the commandant knows what she's doing. There's no need for alarm." Pursey patted his second in command on the back.

Moyer relaxed his tight shoulder muscles a little. "You'd think I'd know by now. But the Denebians put the fear of God in me!"

Lee stood watching the images. "Fear of God is a good trait for all of us, Major Moyer." She picked up a laser pointer. "When the *Daystar* reaches this position—" she aimed the pointer at a spot away from Denebian space "—have the Magnums stand down and return to their patrol positions."

Moyer studied the map and the timetable of the ten Denebian cruisers. "Commandant, the ten cruisers will have formed up with the twenty-five destroyers by then."

Lee responded, "That's my plan. I want the Denebians to think this is serious. It's the only chance that Edge and his crew have to rescue our two cadets. Follow my orders to the letter."

"Aye, sir," both officers responded.

Both men respected Lee's military judgment. She

was an expert tactician. More than once she had saved Intergalactic Command from the ravages of war.

Not having all the information, Moyer dared ask another question of their leader. "Commandant—" his face was creased with worry lines "—one more thing . . ."

"Go ahead," she responded evenly.

"Even if the Denebians don't attack the *Daystar*, what about Irons? He's bound to have security systems in place in the Pegasus Sector. How will Edge get to Irons's headquarters?"

"That's a good question, Matt. Do you want to answer him, Captain?" She smiled at Pursey.

"Matt, every security system has a back door. We have them. Everybody has them. Sometimes there are several back doors. Edge is knowledgeable of the locations of several back doors through Sir Richard's security."

"What if they get caught? We know the kind of revenge that pirate exacts. What do we do then?"

"As far as Intergalactic Command is concerned—nothing. *Daystar* has no official orders from us. She's on her own."

11

Memories—Good and Bad

Raina St. Clair and Mei-Lani Lao enjoyed the exercise room.

That is, they enjoyed it when Lt. Tara Jaleel was not there to torment them with impossible exercises and practice in the martial arts. They came at this hour because Mei-Lani had learned this was the time of day that Jaleel spent in meditation.

The two girls laughed and giggled a great deal as they exercised. At the moment, they were doing an aerobic dance to a strange strain of music.

"What *is* that crazy music you've got on, Mei-Lani?" Raina panted. Her face and body were wet with sweat, and the light blue exercise suit she wore was soaked.

"It's a song called 'Sweet Georgia Brown.'"

"What does *that* mean?" Raina asked in bewilderment.

"It's just an old song from Earth that I dredged up out of the archives. There was a fun basketball team called the Globetrotters. They always warmed up for their act with this song. It's pretty catchy, isn't it?" She was wearing a maroon velour workout suit and was not even breathing hard. Strangely enough, the smaller girl had more stamina than Raina.

"I've got to quit," Raina gasped. "I can't keep up with that silly music." She crossed the padded floor and plopped herself down against the wall. There she picked up a towel, wiped her face, and sat watching as Mei-Lani speeded up the tempo. The girl's feet and hands were literally flying as she accompanied the music.

When the recording ended, she joined Raina. "That was fun," she said. "I like to do aerobics. I just hate all that Jain Jayati."

"I hate it, too. Martial arts are a pain. Of course, if we were as good at it as Dai, maybe it would be fun." Her eyes turned dreamy, and she smiled. "Just think. If we were as fast and strong as he is, we could give Tara as much grief as she gives us."

"I feel so sorry for Lieutenant Jaleel," Mei-Lani said quietly. "She studies that Eastern philosophy all the time, and she's completely under the influence of that Shiva goddess."

A shiver ran over Raina St. Clair as she thought of how evil Shiva was and how completely the goddess dominated the weapons officer.

"I know. I've worried about her a lot. There must be some way that we can help her escape from that evil influence."

"Well, Ringo didn't help any when he bought that Shiva figurine and brought it aboard the *Daystar*."

"I don't think that can cause any more trouble than the big Shiva statue that Lieutenant Jaleel already has in her room. Have you ever seen that?"

"No, and I'm surprised that you have."

"I went there once to give her a message from the bridge. When she opened the door, I saw it." Raina shut her eyes and then her lips for a moment, remembering the obscene statue that seemed to dominate the lieutenant's cabin. "I know it's just a piece of metal or something, but that statue is the symbol for something else. There's something really evil behind Shiva the idol."

"Well, the Bible doesn't make any secret about the fact that Satan's influence is real." Then Mei-Lani fell silent for a while, too. "I've been thinking about Ringo," she began again. "I think he isn't following after the Lord more strongly because he blames God for all the hurt he's been through."

"He has had a horrible life. Why don't we pray for him right now?"

The two girls prayed for some time. First, that God would strengthen Ringo. Second, that He would save Tara Jaleel. Last, they asked the Lord to rid the *Daystar* of the influence of Shiva. Finally they rose and headed for the showers.

After they had showered and dressed, Raina asked, "Mei-Lani, would you mind helping me with something?"

"With what, Raina?"

"I thought it would be nice to have a surprise party for Ringo."

"Why, that's a great idea!" Mei-Lani smiled and gave Raina a hug. "You have a kind heart, Raina, and we ought to show more love to Ringo."

Raina returned the hug and said, "We'll do it, then. We'll do it up right. Only we can't let Heck in on planning the refreshments. He'd have Snickers bars and chocolate sundaes till we'd all die of them!"

Captain Edge was meeting with Zeno Thrax and Ivan Petroski, his first officer and his chief engineer.

Thrax, a perfect albino with white hair and colorless eyes, was in fact an excellent first officer and a generous and kind individual. He came from the planet Mentor Seven, where all the people lived underground and where all were albinos. For some reason that he never revealed, Zeno was an outcast from his native land.

Frowning now, the first officer said solemnly, "We're very close to the Cygnus Sector, sir. Too close, in fact. There have been many ships demolished that were farther away than we are."

"That's right, Captain. We'd better pull away," Petroski put in. "I've heard some bad things about these Denebians."

"You've heard about the Swanson incident, haven't you?" Thrax asked Ivan.

"Who hasn't? Ambassador Swanson's ship was captured by the Denebians," Ivan recounted. "The whole crew was massacred. The Denebians sent Ambassador Swanson's head to Commandant Lee on a magnesium platter."

Captain Edge nodded briefly. "I know that Cygnus is forbidden space, and we won't get any closer than we have to."

Ivan thought this over and looked approving. Then he said, "Well, the *Daystar* is ready for flight."

"Everything running smoothly, Chief?"

"Yes sir. The Mark V engines are running at one hundred and ten percent just in case we need to outrun those Denebians."

At another mention of the Denebians, Zeno Thrax looked uncomfortable again. That was unusual for him, the captain thought, for he was a very steady individual as a rule.

"What's the matter with you, First?" Edge asked. "You look like you'd swallowed a snake!"

"Well, Captain—I do have some bad memories of these people."

"The Denebians?"

"Yes."

"Have you ever personally encountered any of them?"

"As a matter of fact, I have. Back before I left Mentor Seven, they sent a raiding party there. They kidnapped some of our people."

"You never told me that," Ivan Petroski said.

"I don't talk about it much. It's very unpleasant."

"Well, what sort of people are they?"

Zeno shifted his feet nervously. "They're just plain frightening. As you know, all my people live underground in caves and deep mines. We're used to the darkness. And when the Denebians came, most of our people were frightened out of their wits." He looked down at his feet and muttered, "I was myself."

Knowing Zeno Thrax to be a courageous man, Mark Edge exchanged glances with Petroski. "What were they really like, then, Zeno?" he asked gently.

"Well, they're definitely human, but they glow in the dark. They give off a greenish color almost like a green fluorescent light burning." He shivered and said, "I don't even like to think about it."

They glow in the dark, Edge mused. "What's the scientific explanation for *that?*" he wondered aloud.

"Some believe," Zeno Thrax said, "that the star Deneb is so close to its giant gaseous planets that their DNA has mutated. Thus the green glow. But I'm not sure that's true."

"Well, I'd just as soon not meet any of them face to face myself," Edge muttered.

"That goes double for me," Ivan Petroski said. "It sounds like meeting a ghost."

Zeno Thrax's pale eyes studied the chunky chief engineer. "They're worse than ghosts, Ivan," he said quietly. Then he turned and left the bridge.

"I never knew Zeno to get spooked by anything," Petroski muttered. "If *he's* afraid of those people, there's something to be afraid of."

"Well, I agree with you, for Zeno's a brave man. But we're all afraid of something, I guess. Whatever the Denebians are, I've got the feeling that sooner or later we're going to meet up with some of them."

Ivan looked through the forward viewer. "Deneb is

such a handsome star to have a race like the Denebians on one of its planets' moons." The dwarf was making adjustments to his datacorder. "Captain, did you know that Deneb is over one hundred thousand times larger than Earth's sun?"

"As a matter of fact, I do! Also, I know that it has six gaseous giant planets, each almost as big as Earth's solar system. And for another thing, each giant planet has moons orbiting around it, and only a few are inhabitable."

Ivan was impressed with the captain's knowledge.

Edge laughed. "Ivan, I used to fly around here all the time when I worked for Irons. Cygnus is an old friend of mine. And I much prefer the star Matar in Pegasus to Deneb. On a clear night in the Matar System, you can see the spiral-armed galaxy of NGC 7331 just to the northwest. Scientists believe that NGC 7331 looks very much like the Milky Way. It gives us a good idea how our own galaxy might appear from a distance of fifty million light-years."

Ivan appeared to be pondering something as he continued to study Cygnus. "Captain, do you think there are other intelligent civilizations out there? I mean, in the twentieth century, many people on Earth thought that there must be other races or species out in space." He looked up at Edge. "Star Drive was discovered several thousand years ago, and man has colonized many planets, but we've never discovered any of those aliens that people believed in."

Edge rubbed his foot along the seam of the blue carpet under his feet. "I don't know, Ivan. I've thought about that myself. If they're out here, they sure have done a good job at covering their tracks. We still do not have one shred of evidence that confirms alien existence. I guess the bottom line is that we'll never know until we run into one of them."

Ivan examined the data on the star charts. "I don't see one Denebian ship headed in our direction, Captain."

"Very good. Change heading for Matar. Let me know the moment we're within two sectors of it." The captain left the bridge and headed toward sick bay.

Seated by the large portal in the recreation lounge, Bronwen Llewellen and Dai gazed quietly at the Cygnus constellation. Dai loved his aunt and respected her judgment. Her knowledge of the galaxy was staggering. Few persons in the intergalactic community had spent more time traveling the stars. As she looked deeply into Cygnus, her eyes welled up with tears.

Dai, sensing her mood, asked, "What's wrong, Aunt Bronwen?"

"Nothing is wrong, Dai. I was just thinking—I'm one of the few people who has ever traveled in Denebian space and lived to tell about it." She took her handkerchief from her pocket and wiped her eyes.

"You've actually been there? But you've never said anything about it!"

"True."

"It's got to be one of your most exciting stories. And you don't share it? How come?" Dai was beside himself with curiosity.

"I'm almost fifty-three years old now. I was twenty-five when I made the journey."

Bronwen stood and moved closer to the portal, and Dai followed.

"The Northern Cross. That's what we called the constellation."

"We who?" Dai interrupted.

"A friend." She paused. "He was one of the most godly men I ever knew. I met him aboard a ship called the *Orient*—at a prayer meeting we had in the ship's chapel."

"Wasn't the *Orient* one of the liners that was destroyed by the Denebians?"

"*Utterly* destroyed is how I would phrase it!" Bronwen said. Her face was dark from the memory, and tears started welling up in her eyes again. "I was a brand-new navigator aboard a brand-new luxury liner. She was the most advanced ship of her time. People bragged that not even God could scuttle her. She was advertised as the safest deep-space passenger liner in existence."

"And what about the man?"

"As I said, that man had the closest relationship with Jesus Christ of anyone that I had ever known." Bronwen reached over and brushed Dai's hair back out of his eyes. "He was humble as well as wise. When I looked into his eyes, it was if I could see into heaven itself." She turned back toward the portal. "You have eyes like him, Dai. He had a special calling on his life, and so do you!"

"But what happened to him?" Dai asked. He stayed at his aunt's side, looking through the cruiser's portal at the Northern Cross.

"Let me start at the beginning. The *Orient* was headed toward a star by the name of Zeta Cygni." She pointed. "See it. It's just south of Sadr on a line through Epsilon Cygni."

Dai looked and nodded.

"Zeta Cygni has a tremendous view of the double star Albireo."

"I think Albireo is one of the most beautiful double stars in the galaxy," the boy said. "All gold and blue."

Bronwen smiled at him. "I believe that everyone aboard *Orient* would have agreed with you. Well, I was young then, and Albireo had a romantic effect on me."

"Why, Aunt Bronwen!"

She laughed. "I haven't been fifty-two all my life,

young man. And back then I did turn a man's head once in a while."

"Oh." Dai looked at his aunt in a new light. "Well, OK. So the *Orient* is headed toward a colony at Zeta Cygni," he reminded her.

"Remember, we were told we were safe aboard an indestructible ship."

Bronwen sat back down, and Dai joined her. She pointed to another section of Cygnus.

"I know what that is—it's Cygnus X-1. A black hole that emits radio waves. Its emissions were the first picked up by early Earth astronomers." Dai bit his upper lip as he looked at the long spiral arms of black matter that were falling into the black hole.

"Well, the captain decided to impress our passengers, and he piloted the ship closer to the black hole than he should have. We got caught in the initial gravity pull. He ordered the engines to full speed. The ship was propelled by eight Dynoptic Star Thruster engines."

"Eight Star Thrusters!" Dai moved to the edge of his seat. "That engine would have been twice as big as *Daystar*'s!"

"It took a lot of power to move a star liner that size," she said. "Those big engines strained so hard that we all felt we were going to have our internal organs shaken right out of us. But the ship was not breaking free. I remember the captain's face. He was terrified. When I saw his face, I thought we were done for. And then it happened."

"What?" Dai asked. He was completely engrossed in the story.

"A big chunk of that dark matter that spirals around the black hole hit the stern of the ship. The engines were gone, and the only thing that saved us was the inertia stabilizers. But the explosion blew us at light speed straight toward one of the biggest stars in the galaxy."

"How'd you stop the ship?"

"We didn't. The Denebians did! Several of their star cruisers were on patrol when we shot by them. They powered up, caught up to us, and then tractored the liner to their home world."

"I bet everyone was relieved."

"Not at all. The Denebians were and still are the fiercest people known to our star systems. We had jumped out of the frying pan and into the fire, as they used to say in the twentieth century." Bronwen went to the dispenser to get a glass of water. "You want one?"

"Please," he said gratefully. His eyes were as large as silver dollars. "What an adventure! You could write a book about this, Aunt."

Bronwen returned to the couch and gave Dai his drink. "The Denebians transferred all of us onto their ships. I watched in dismay as they pulverized the *Orient* into microscopic particles."

"What do these people look like? I've heard rumors they look like spooks."

"They are human beings, except that they glow in a strange green light. Scientists have speculated. Maybe it's something chemical that is unique to their part of the universe. No one really knows. The glow is unnerving enough in daylight, but at night their appearance filled us with sheer terror." She took a sip of water. "And I think that whatever causes the green glow also is affecting their minds. They enjoy only their own company. Any outsiders are hated with extreme malice."

"Do you think they would make war with us?"

"They are formidable enemies. Fortunately, they are content to stay in the Cygnus Sector for the most part. They do send out raiding parties from time to time. They seem to lean toward kidnapping. And they don't like anyone trespassing on their star space." She finished drinking and set down her glass on the table beside her.

"What happened next?"

"We were split up into groups of twenty. Groups of us were sent to different cities on their home world. My friend and the captain and I were in the same group. We were taken to the capital city." Bronwen's voice cracked as she continued. "There we learned we were to be sacrificed to their goddess, Astarte. They took us to her temple."

Bronwen stood again. "The chief priest of the temple ordered us thrown into the fire in the name of Astarte. Everyone started screaming when they took hold of us —except for the man. His face was full of peace and joy. It was like looking into the face of an angel. I'll never forget it."

Dai got up and put an arm around his aunt's waist.

"In a loud voice he gave testimony to the gospel of Jesus Christ. The Denebians seemed unable to move a muscle until he finished. He offered to lead them to salvation. Those were the last words he ever spoke. Then *she* came down from the altar of Astarte and ran him through with a golden spear. He died with the same angelic expression on his face. I thought of the early Christians who died in the coliseums in Rome. Historians note that they had smiles on their faces."

"Who was 'she'?"

"Zaria," Bronwen replied soberly. "The same Zaria we encountered on the planet Morlandria. A quite young Zaria, but Zaria just the same."

"Zaria!"

"It's apparent she has done nothing but grow in evil ever since. She was not content to stay in the Cygnus

Sector. So eventually she traveled to Morlandria to align that whole planet with Astarte. I'm convinced her ultimate goal is to rule the whole galaxy."

"How did *you* escape?"

"That is a very good question. It looked hopeless. I was praying and letting the Lord know that I was coming very soon. Then an earthquake shook the entire structure. Huge blocks of stone began falling everywhere. Our guards ran. One entire wall of the temple crumbled. And on the other side of it sat a small corvette not much bigger than *Daystar.* Our rescue ship."

Dai scratched his head in wonder. "It was just docked there?"

"While the man gave his testimony, I told you that none of the Denebians seemed able to move."

"Right."

"*We* could still move, but most of us were petrified by what was going on. Only the captain thought quickly enough to seize his opportunity, and he slipped away. When we were brought to the temple, he'd seen that corvette nearby in the docking bay of a rich Denebian. He powered it up and rescued us. We were out of the Cygnus Sector before their patrolling cruisers knew what happened."

"The other man. Your friend. What was his name, Aunt?" Dai asked.

"The man's name . . . I did know what it was . . . I have no doubt of that. It's just that I can't remember it." She pointed her right index finger to her head. "It's up here, but somehow I can't get at the information. I've lain awake nights trying to think of it. Maybe I'm not *supposed* to remember it."

Dai smiled as he looked lovingly at his aunt. "Well, if you do remember, write it down, and then call for me ASAP!"

12

Secret Orders

Raina St. Clair's mind was a million miles away as she walked toward the dining hall. In fact, she was so preoccupied that she ran headlong into Heck.

The instant she rammed into his back, he let out a bloodcurdling yell and whirled, his face red with anger.

"Oh, Heck, I'm so sorry! I know your back is still sore!"

Actually, Ringo had told her Heck's back was killing him, and the bump by Raina must have been very painful.

But Heck would never have admitted such a thing. "Why, sweetheart," he said, "it was nothing at all. You just startled me a little bit, that's all." He walked along with her.

"I know it's more than that," Raina said. "Ringo told me you're black and blue from where the lieutenant threw you against that wall."

"Oh, Ringo's always overstating things!"

Raina smiled, for it was Heck who always overstated things. He had a way of imputing his own faults to others. But despite herself and despite Heck, she had learned to like the red-haired boy.

"I'm a lot stronger than most people think I am," Heck bragged. "Look at this muscle." Stripping back the sleeve of his tunic, he brought up his fist in the classic muscle-making position to show his biceps. In truth he was a strong young man, but the muscle was covered with a thick layer of fat. "I'm a lot stronger than everybody thinks," he repeated. "Just feel that muscle."

Mei-Lani caught up with them just then. She glanced at Raina, and suddenly the two girls began laughing. They went into the chow hall and started toward a table.

Heck yelled after them, "I'm just too much man for you girls! That's the problem with you!"

"That's right. Too much man! That's the problem!" Raina called back, then she and Mei-Lani went off into another fit of giggling.

"I don't think you handled that right."

Studs Cagney, the crew chief, came up behind Heck. Cagney was a short, muscular man with thinning black hair and very dark, penetrating eyes. He worked his crew hard and was able to whip any of them—except Dai Bando, whom nobody could whip.

"What do you mean I handled it wrong? What do you know about it, Studs?"

"Well, some girls might like that he-man stuff, but not those two. You'd be better off if you'd just keep it honest with them."

"All girls like a guy to show off a little bit."

"Not those two." Cagney shook his head confidently. "They're different. They've got something in them that's different from most everyone I've ever met."

Heck stared at the crew chief, seemingly puzzled by his words. "You're not getting religion, are you, Chief?"

Cagney looked at him for a moment, then said, "I might be. I need some. I've led a tough life."

Studs had always been a rough, brutal man. The crew chief had once attempted to rough up Dai Bando, though, and had suddenly found himself flat on his back, handled as easily as if he were a child. He had been humiliated. However, Dai had a gentle spirit. And the boy had put himself out to show Studs that he wanted to be a good worker.

"I'm interested in the brand of religion that Dai and his aunt, the navigator, have. It's the real thing."

"Aw, that's for sissies, Studs! You ought to know that!"

Studs turned his weathered face toward the boy. "When you've been around Neptune as many times as I have, kid, you'll find out this world is not as much fun as you think."

"I still say let's not get serious about this. Come on. Let's get something to eat."

He followed the young Ranger into the dining area. He watched as Heck loaded his plate with huge portions of everything that was offered on the food line. "You eat too much."

"A man needs to keep his strength up! A man needs nourishment, Studs."

Studs was a hearty eater himself, but he did hard physical work and burned it off, whereas Heck sat at a computer all day and amused himself by eating candy bars.

"One of these days," Studs said, "all that extra weight's going to catch up with you."

"Like how?"

"Well, you're going to try to run away from something like a Melacondran dragon. They're pretty fast, you know, and you'd make a juicy mouthful for them."

"Never worry about things like that," Heck said breezily as they sat down with their trays. "The way I figure it, the more of me there is, the more there is for the girls to love. Right, Studs?"

"Wrong," the chief said and shook his head sadly.

Bronwen Llewellen's quarters were sparse in furnishings, and there weren't any of the usual mementos that adorned most of the crew's quarters.

117

There's a Spartan quality about her cabin, Dai thought, and he was reminded of the training, self-discipline, and self-denial of the ancient warriors. He looked around, noting a bed with simple coverings, three chairs, two tables, and a closet. Her Bible rested at the center of the larger table along with a cup that contained six red pens.

"Try this drink, Dai," Bronwen said as she sat down at the table with her favorite nephew.

Dai took a sip, and a smile crossed his face. "This tastes great! What is it?"

"I put a little apricot and nectarine juice in with some melon juice. Mixed them all together, and this is it. Pretty good, if you ask me."

While downing the rest of the drink, Dai said. "It's the best-tasting fruit punch I've had in a long time." He wiped his mouth on his sleeve. "Can I have some more?"

Getting up to refill his glass, Bronwen gave him a stern look. "Dai, I would expect that sort of behavior from anyone on the ship but you!"

"What?" he asked innocently. "What'd I do?"

"I never want to see you wipe your mouth with your sleeve again. I can see Heck doing that sort of thing all day long. Use your napkin!"

Looking down at his soiled sleeve, Dai nodded respectfully but took no offense. Something was on his mind.

His aunt gave him his refill and sat back down.

"Aunt," Dai said, "I'm very curious about something. Did you ever go back to Deneb space?"

"You're a very perceptive young man." She put her hand on his head and mussed his hair. "Yes, I went one other time—with Ambassador Swanson."

"Ambassador Swanson!" Dai ran his fingers through his mussed hair, trying to straighten it out. "The one who was murdered by the Denebians and his head was sent back to Commandant Lee on a platter?"

"The very one."

Dai situated his body on his chair for the most comfort. "Please tell me the story."

Bronwen didn't seem eager to repeat the account, but she didn't refuse her nephew's request, either. "A few years after the *Orient* disaster, I went to work for Intergalactic Command. I was older than most new hires, but I had more light-years under my belt than most, and they needed a knowledgeable navigator for a special mission."

"And it was to the Denebian planets. How could you possibly want to go back there?"

Bronwen began fiddling with the red pens. "I had no idea we were going there. I never dreamed of the possibility of going back. I didn't think anyone would."

There was a barking at the door. Dai got up and opened it, and Contessa strolled in. She promptly sat down on the floor beside Bronwen.

His aunt continued. "Our passenger was Ambassador Swanson. He carried a special folder with the Intergalactic seal covering the face of it. Commandant Lee had instructed our captain to proceed to Pegasus and await further orders."

"I would have been nervous already, knowing that I was headed anywhere near Deneb."

"I had no choice. I'd signed up for duty, and I was bound by my oath."

"OK, then what?"

"We were approaching the star Algenib in the Pegasus Sector when Ambassador Swanson broke the seal on the folder and handed Captain Mears the contents. The captain's face dropped to the floor. He had been ordered by the Council to travel to the forest moon of Copan. Copan was Denebian. It orbited one of the giant green gas planets in the Cygnus Sector."

Dai could understand the gravity of the situation. "It's a wonder the crew didn't mutiny. Those orders are like sentencing everyone aboard to certain death!"

"That's where Ambassador Swanson's unique abilities came in. He was an accomplished diplomat. Whether the problem was with worlds, or nations, or just a few people, he had the extraordinary ability to bring peaceful resolutions to conflicts. He believed that if he could spend some time with the Denebians, he could convince them to form an alliance with Intergalactic Command. He convinced us that our participation was essential to the success of the mission and persuaded us to carry out our duties as we had been trained to do. And we did. I never was prouder of any other crew. They were the very definition of professionalism."

"I don't think I could have been. The stories about the Denebians are pretty gross."

"Never forget one thing, Dai. God will never give you more than you can handle. Some things may seem too much, but they're really not—it just *feels* like it at the time." She gently patted her Bible. "Don't base your decisions on your feelings but on this Book. That's why you need to get His Word into yourself. Know it thoroughly from front to back. Know it so well that if anyone quotes something incorrect from it, you'll see the mistake immediately."

Suddenly the German shepherd got up. She placed her paws on the table and began sniffing at Bronwen's fruit drink.

"I should never have given her a bowl of this. Now this big black dog won't leave me alone." She went to the counter and poured some apricot nectarine melon juice into a dish. Holding up the gallon container, she said to Contessa. "You could drink this whole thing, couldn't you?"

Contessa's eyes sparkled as she saw the fruit juice waving in the air.

"This is enough for now. Someone needs to watch your weight. I think Heck's candy bars are putting a little weight on *you*."

Contessa whimpered as she lapped up the sweet juice.

With the dog occupied, Bronwen came back to the table and began toying with the cup containing the red pens.

"What are the pens for? I didn't think anyone wrote by hand anymore. It's easier to speak into the computer."

"Very true." She gazed for a moment at the pens. "These were given to me by an old brother in the Lord just before he died. His name was John Mitchell."

"I've never heard you mention that name. Who was he?"

Bronwen pursed her lips, then said, "My life has been very full, and there are a good many things I haven't told anyone—including you, nephew!"

Dai grimaced, but a small smile tried to etch its way across his face.

"Years ago, Brother Mitchell lived out in the wilds of Arkansas. Some of us traveled light-years out of our way to visit him, for we enjoyed his Bible studies. He lived in a small cabin at the end of a dirt road that wasn't even on the map. And you know how I love maps!"

She took one of the red pens from the cup. "When we walked in, he would greet us, point to a seat by the table, and tell us to use one of his red pens. He believed people should write notes in their Bibles during a Bible study. This same procedure occurred every time someone visited him." She opened her Bible and flipped to several different passages. Each had been underlined in red.

Dai pondered Brother Mitchell for a moment. "He must have been a good teacher."

"I don't think he would have thought of himself that way. Although all the rest of us did!" Bronwen kept turning pages as if each one held a special memory. "He went blind, and his wife would read the Bible to him. He would memorize whole books—chapter and verse! It was the only way he could study the Bible, since he couldn't see to read."

Dai began wishing that he had met Brother Mitchell.

"I went to several of his studies. One of my regrets in life is that I didn't spend more time with him. I've never met another man like him in all my travels."

"And he's not living now?"

"No. I heard that he was sick, but it took me several weeks to get back to Earth. He had died by the time I arrived. He left these red pens for me with a note telling me to continue reading God's Word and marking what God shows me with a red pen. So I do."

"I wish I would have met him." Dai's face was sober.

Bronwen laughed out loud. "I have no doubt but that you'll meet him in heaven. I can picture the two of you hopping from mountaintop to mountaintop, shouting 'glory' at the top of your lungs!"

"Bridge to navigator," the intercom blared.

"Bronwen here, Raina."

"Captain Edge needs to see you up on the bridge at once."

"On my way," Bronwen responded. "Dai, we'll have to finish the ambassador's story later." She started for the door, and he followed.

They parted company in the corridor. Dai's own duty time was coming up, and he needed to report to Ivan Petroski.

13

Through the Minefields

Captain Edge and Zeno Thrax sat in the small conference room that connected to the *Daystar*'s bridge. Edge used this room only when he wanted to have a conversation in complete privacy. When the door to *this* conference room closed, the whole crew was filled with curiosity.

The captain and Thrax had been in there for some time.

Zeno was studying the Pegasus Sector on the star map. The albino's eyes turned to slits as he considered the strategic placement of the space mines surrounding the Earth-sized moon Palenque, which circled the gaseous planet Olmec.

"The placement of the minefields around Palenque makes unauthorized access to Irons's headquarters impossible," Thrax deduced. "I've studied this from every conceivable angle, and there is *no* way to navigate in this space without being blown to microns by the space mines."

Edge stood next to his white, almost translucent second in command. They looked at each other for a moment. Being highly intuitive, almost to the point of mind reading, Zeno was sure the captain was holding back information from him.

The effect of Thrax's colorless eyes was unnerving —some would say terrifying—to most naturally pigmented human beings. But Mark Edge and Zeno had been friends for many years. The captain was neither unnerved nor terrified.

"There is a way," Edge answered matter-of-factly.

"Well, I can't figure it out. These minefields are three-dimensional death traps. It is impossible for a ship to fly clear of one mine without detonating the next one to it." Thrax moved the star map and adjusted it to different angles. "Irons has constructed the most elaborate defense system that I have ever seen."

The captain pointed to an area on the star chart. "Here's where the *Jackray* got through." He adjusted a control switch, and the map highlighted a corridor through the minefield. "As you can see, the space mines have been deactivated along this corridor to allow the ship access to the moon's docking station."

Edge brushed his hair back from his forehead and adjusted the infrared setting on the star map. Several mines on the map turned from red to blue. "As soon as the *Jackray* cleared the minefield, the mines reactivated, turning from blue back to red on the map."

Thrax was frustrated. "I hate it when you decide to play guessing games with me. If you know how to get to Irons's headquarters, why don't you just tell me?"

Edge laughed. "Zeno, you are so serious most of the time. Usually, *you're* the one with the answers. This is one of those times when I'm the one with the answer."

He revolved the entire star map until they were looking at the side of the moon opposite Sir Richard's massive headquarters.

Thrax moved closer to the screen.

Much of the surface here was covered with water. And much of the water was covered by huge storm systems. Swirling megahurricanes spun like tops across the surface.

"This is the Ocean of Storms," Edge told him.

Lightning flashed across the viewer like multiple fireworks shot into the sky with rockets. The captain adjusted the viewer so that they could see the ocean floor. Huge caverns pocketed the entire length and breadth of it.

"One and only one cavern travels through the moon to the other side."

"And you just happen to know which one it is." Thrax pointed to a likely possibility. "I think it's this one."

Edge grinned. "So did I—at first. Believe me, the big ones are all a waste of time. But there is one that goes all the way through the center of the moon to the bottom of Irons's headquarters on the other side." Edge moved to his left. "You see this little one?"

"You mean the one with two pillars on either side of it?"

The captain answered calmly. "Those pillars are two thousand feet high and are named Titan's Troubles. I'm pretty sure they were named after the Titan's Twins formation on Earth." He magnified the cavern entrance, located directly behind Titan's Troubles. "This cavern opens up into a tunnel that passes through the center of Palenque. The entrance is called Titan's Voice because the water that travels through it makes a moaning sound."

"I assume the tunnel has a name?" Zeno asked.

"Of course, just like everything else on this moon. The tunnel is Titan's Way. I know of no other planet-sized body in space that has a naturally formed tunnel extending through it."

"Not even Mentor Seven has a naturally occurring tunnel like that—although we have *dug* tunnels through the length and breadth of it." Thrax looked with admiration at the moon. "So where does Titan's Way go?"

"We enter here at Titan's Troubles," Edge said, tracing the path on the star map with his right forefinger. "Then we maneuver inside Titan's Voice and travel through Titan's Way until we reach a gigantic cavern located directly under Sir Richard's headquarters."

"May I assume the cavern is named after Titan somehow?" Thrax asked.

Edge chuckled. "Actually, no. This cavern was one of the first to be discovered on Palenque, and it's no accident that Irons built his headquarters over the top of it. It was many years later before anyone discovered Titan's Troubles."

"So the cavern is named what?"

Edge tugged at the front of his tunic, straightening it. "The Grotto of Nioux."

"What a strange name!" Thrax exclaimed. "Why that?"

"It's named after a cavern located in France back on Earth. That's a huge rotunda decorated with primitive paintings from early in Earth's history."

"So this cavern must have paintings, too."

"All over it! Except that these paintings are a history of the Irons family dynasty instead of primitive artwork. Thousands of years of Irons family history are represented on those walls. The Ironses have always been the ruling family on this moon. And, for the most part, they have been gracious and kindly to their people. Their latest leader—Sir Richard—he's the black sheep of the family."

Zeno studied the twin towers of Titan's Troubles. "Doesn't look to me like a ship could get through here."

"Not a big one for sure, but one the size of *Daystar* could."

Thrax then examined the ocean floor. There was nothing to indicate that this cavern entrance led to a secret tunnel leading in turn straight to Irons's headquarters. "It will be heavily mined."

Edge shook his head. "Not a single mine." The captain began reminiscing. "No one but three people know the existence of this tunnel. Of course, Sir Richard knows about it—it's his escape route in case things go bad for him at his headquarters."

"And obviously *you* know about it. So that's two. Who's the third?"

"Francesca Del Ray."

Zeno looked at the floor for a moment. His eyes narrowed. "I wonder how she knows. Because she's his second?"

"No. While Irons was away to attend a council meeting, he left Francesca in charge. She took the time to download his databases into her computer. While going over his files, she discovered his escape route." Edge flexed his arms in the air above him. "In fact, she's the one who showed the escape route to me."

"Why in the name of Pluto would she do that? That woman is every bit as evil as Irons. Even on Mentor Seven, she has the reputation of being a Corbrin viper, and that's the most venomous creature on my home world."

"Not to mention, the ugliest. I hate snakes as it is, but snakes that have tails with poisonous barbs on them are more than I want to handle. Come to think of it, they are a lot like Francesca. Though you'll have to admit—Francesca is anything but ugly."

"Mark, I don't like this mission." When the two men were alone, Thrax often felt at liberty to call the captain by his first name. "The last thing you need is to get near Del Ray again. You know Irons. The man's vengeful. He never forgets an offense—even if it *is* all in his imagination."

"I've thought of that, but no one can get us to his headquarters but me. Titan's Way is too complicated to draw a map. Too many tunnels lead off of it."

Zeno studied the star map again. "Making a journey underwater through the center of that moon is one thing, but how will we even get to the moon? I still say Irons's minefields make it impossible."

"There is a back door. And I know where it is."

"You don't have to tell me—Francesca Del Ray again."

"When I was a captain for Irons, I met Francesca during a meeting at headquarters. She was . . . attentive. And I didn't have sense enough to back away," Edge continued. "I wasn't interested in her, but I was flattered by her attention. It's something that I now regret. Irons became extremely jealous. He tried to kill me, but I avoided his efforts somehow. I knew I needed to get off the moon quick. Francesca offered to help me. I later discovered that her motives weren't entirely unmixed." Edge's face darkened.

"How's that?" Zeno asked.

"She had heard Irons bragging about the tridium and how rich it would make him. I was the only one who knew where Makon and the tridium were. She felt that if she confided the secret of his escape route to me, I would be obligated to tell her where Makon was."

"Does Irons know this?"

"Absolutely not! He would kill her if he knew that she revealed his escape route to me."

"So Francesca was helping Irons locate the tridium."

"Francesca was helping Francesca. She wanted the tridium for herself. My good sense took a vacation, and I fell for all the attention."

"The next part of the story is the part I know about."

"Yes, that's when you became a very good friend." Edge's eyes reflected gratitude.

"I'd just left Mentor Seven. I was ready for a friend myself."

The captain jumped on the opportunity to turn the conversation away from himself. "You know, you've never told me what happened on Mentor Seven, Zeno."

Thrax walked to a portal and looked out at the stars. "I will . . . someday. Maybe after this mission—if we live through it." The albino returned to the star map. "Now how do we get through the minefield?"

Edge adjusted the map so that it displayed both Pegasus and Cygnus Sectors. He punched a few buttons, and intersecting lines appeared through the map. Then he flipped open the communications grid. "Captain to navigator," he said.

"Bronwen here, Captain."

"Come to my conference room. We need to chart a course."

"Be there in a moment." Her voice sounded full of peace. It was almost relaxing to hear.

The captain flipped down the grid. "I'm afraid that peaceful, relaxed feeling our navigator has is about to change."

Zeno Thrax nodded in agreement.

Tension aboard *Daystar* was so thick it could be cut with a Neuromag. Bronwen Llewellyn was calculating maneuver after maneuver as the cruiser plunged through space. Not only did the ship have to be in exact locations, but it also had to be at those locations at exact times. These maneuvers were programmed into the central computer cores of the space mines. As long as *Daystar* followed the maze precisely, they would survive the mines. But everybody aboard knew that the next breath could be their last.

Drops of sweat poured from the captain's forehead. "Give me the next maneuver," he said softly. There was no need to shout. The bridge was so quiet that they could have heard a pin drop if it were not for the hum of the computers.

The navigator had dropped all efforts at formality. There wasn't enough time for it. "We're approaching the intersection of Alpheratz with Markab at the northeast diagonal."

"Very good," Edge responded. "Once we clear that point, we should be free of the minefield."

Bronwen started her countdown. "Course change on my mark . . . five . . . four . . . three . . . two . . . one . . . mark!"

Edge brought the nose of *Daystar* around in an arc that finally pointed directly at the Ocean of Storms.

"You have ten seconds to reach the stratosphere," Bronwen warned.

Edge knew—as she knew—that a failure of one second would result in the explosion of the last mine.

But *Daystar* entered Palenque's stratosphere exactly as planned. Edge piloted the ship over three small hurricanes, located in the northeast quadrant of the ocean.

"We better submerge as soon as possible. Irons's security forces could have picked us up," Thrax advised.

"I suppose so, though I doubt it. Bronwen, you better start working on the minefield exit route just in case we have to use it sooner than expected," Edge ordered.

Without responding, the navigator started on the equations needed for their escape.

The captain guided the ship toward the ocean. The crew had never gone directly from space flight to traveling underwater, but it was a trip that the captain had made many times.

Thrax calculated the nautical miles they would need to travel beneath the surface. "If we submerge at this point, we'll still have to travel twenty-five hundred miles to reach Titan's Troubles."

"We don't have a choice. Better to take a little longer hidden underneath the surface than to have the *Jackray* start shooting at us. One hit from her and we'll be nothing more than microns." Edge pulled at his atmospheric stabilizers, and the *Daystar* gently nosed into the Ocean of Storms. "Besides, turbulence from one of the giant hurricanes could break us apart."

The engines of *Daystar* operated as well underwater as they did in the vacuum of outer space. The ship's navigational system brought the cruiser directly to the massive Titan's Troubles.

"Captain," Bronwen said, looking up from her computer console. "The exit route is plotted and recorded on the navigational memory banks."

Edge nodded his head. "Good job, Bronwen. Now we have to get through Titan's Way."

The first officer had been standing beside him. "How are we going to get through *that?*" he asked nervously as he pointed to Titan's Troubles. The two huge pillars stood very close together.

"Relax, Zeno. Look at the base of the pillar on the left."

Zeno leaned forward and followed the left pillar down to its base. Then he whistled softly. The inside bottom of that pillar had been carved wider by ocean currents. The result was space for the ship to pass through Titan's Troubles and enter Titan's Way. "I couldn't see the bottom of the pillars from space," Zeno grunted. "No wonder no one knows about this route."

"Exactly!" The captain flipped open his communications grid. "Heck, I need you up here now."

"Aye, sir."

When Heck appeared, Captain Edge motioned him toward Bronwen. "I need you to help the navigator. One wrong turn in this tunnel, and we're done for."

Heck had engineered a device to emit navigational security scanning beams. There was only one path to the Grotto of Nioux. Heck's instrument would indicate which of the many tunnels to take. The captain couldn't remember every detail of the tunnels and felt a little more secure knowing that, if they did take the wrong tunnel, they might be able to back out of it before the booby traps were tripped.

Heck was his usual boisterous self. "No worries, Captain. Heck is here. It is incredible how sensitive my devices have become." He happily started adjusting the controls of his apparatus.

Edge noted the comment for future reference. He asked himself, *Could I ever have been as overconfident as Heck?* The captain wiped his forehead with a handkerchief. He decided that one of the benefits of being a teenager was the sense of invincibility. It was a sense that he had lost several years ago.

Thrax patted the captain's left shoulder. The albino had no problem reading the captain's thoughts this time.

The *Daystar* came up out of the watery tunnel and entered the huge cavern known as the Grotto of Nioux. A couple of hundred tunnels led from the massive grotto, but Edge remembered the mural painted above the

132

exact tunnel that led to Irons's headquarters. He landed the ship just to the side of the entrance to that tunnel.

The ship's gangway extended to let the crew exit into the rotunda-shaped cavern. The lights of the *Daystar* illumined the cave, making it as bright as day. It was evident that the cavern walls had murals painted on them from one end to the other.

Mei-Lani found her voice first. "These murals are magnificent," she said to Ringo. "They actually tell the story of the Irons family through the last several millenniums."

Ringo studied the mural picturing some red pyramids decorated with green accents. Indeed, the landscape of the mural was dominated by red pyramids. They looked like a large city. He was drawn to one pyramid that was larger than the others. At its top was the relief of a large bird with writing underneath it.

Ringo found himself shaking. He drew his medallion out of his shirt.

"What's the matter, Ringo?" Mei-Lani asked.

"I don't know—maybe nothing. It's just that the large bird in the mural looks a lot like what's on my medallion."

Mei-Lani examined the pyramid on the mural, the relief of the large bird, and the inscription under the bird. "I know it looks like your medallion, but the painting is very aged. Just don't jump to conclusions. I wish I could see more of the writing. We need more words."

Then the captain was calling everyone back to the gangplank, and Raina called, "Let's go. The captain wants us."

Ringo stuck his medallion back into his shirt. A faint feeling of hope started to warm his stomach. *Dear*

Lord, at least show me anything about this place that might have meaning for me, he prayed silently. He gave no thought to Shiva whatsoever.

Just then the far-off sound of blasters filled the air. The cavern shook and dust swirled.

"Over here." The captain was waving his arms toward a tunnel entrance just beyond the ship.

All the Space Rangers fanned out in a semicircle in front of the tunnel opening. They held their Neuromags at the ready. Although the melee sounded as if it was right on top of them, there was no sign of anyone.

Edge shouted above the noise, "The blasters are in the tunnels above us." He pointed his Neuromag toward the ceiling. "Probably around the stockade area."

Then Captain Edge divided the group into teams and gave each team an assignment.

While Edge spoke to Tara Jaleel for a moment, Ringo watched Mei-Lani scan the entire rotunda.

"Let's go, Ringo," she said. "I've recorded all the murals on my datacorder."

"Well, thanks! Make sure you don't let anything happen to it," he cautioned as they ran into the tunnel behind Captain Edge and Tara Jaleel.

After the rescue party had disappeared into the dark passage that led to Sir Richard Irons's headquarters, Bronwen Llewellen and Contessa came down the gangplank and followed them into the darkness.

The Lord be with us, she prayed fervently. *I sense great evil in this place. But I also sense that He wants me there.*

14
Son of Sir Richard

Olga Von Kemp was desperately trying to bring down Karl Bentlow's fever. When she laid her hand on his forehead, it felt almost as if a fire were blazing on the inside. "Oh, Karl," she whispered, "don't die, please don't die!"

At that moment Cadet Von Kemp longed for a God to pray to, but she had none. She had laughed at Christianity, especially when she saw it lived out in the Space Rangers. She remembered now how she had helped throw Raina St. Clair bodily out of the Academy. For some reason, regret washed through her.

As she dipped a cloth into the tepid water left by the guard and began to moisten Bentlow's dry, chapped lips, Olga whimpered, "Oh, why doesn't somebody come to help us?"

At that moment she heard a loud noise just outside the cell. She leaped to her feet and rushed across the room. Stopping just short of the security field protecting the cell's doorway, Olga could feel the energy discharge emanating from its invisible beams. The hair on her head started to react to the static electricity and rose from her head in all directions. She pressed her face to the small barred window located to the door's right, but she could see very little.

Then suddenly the muzzle of a Neuromag appeared, and a guard snarled, "Get away from that opening, or I'll blast you!"

But even while he was speaking, a bright explosion knocked the door free from its hinges and slammed the guard against the opposing wall. His body slumped—lifelessly, it seemed—to the stone floor.

Olga screamed as three troopers entered, all clothed in body armor. She thought that it was an execution squad sent to kill them, and she threw herself over Karl's body, shrieking, "Don't! Don't kill us!"

One of the intruders lifted his face mask. "Stop that screaming, Olga—you're all right!"

Olga looked up wildly and was shocked when she saw the face of Jerusha Ericson. "Jerusha!" she whispered, "what are you doing here?"

"We've come to get you out of here! Now, stand up!" She knelt quickly beside Karl, then nodded to her two companions. "Zeno, you and Dai will have to carry Karl."

"We'd better do it fast," Dai said. He came forward and by himself picked up the still form of the sick boy. "They'll be after us soon."

"Karl needs a doctor," Olga said in a whisper. She could not believe what was happening. "How did you find us?"

"By the message you left on the corvette, and Captain Edge knew the way," Zeno said. "Now, we've got to get out of here."

"Where's Zaria?" Jerusha demanded, staring around the gloomy cell. "Is she kept in another place?"

"She was in here with us for a while," Olga said. "She started flirting with one of the guards, and he let her out. But I think she killed him. I'm sure she killed him."

"That must have been the guard we found dead down the corridor," Zeno said.

"Where could she have gone?" Dai asked. He was holding the limp body of Bentlow easily.

"My guess is she's gone after Irons. She hates him.

That's all she's been talking about in here. She wants to destroy him."

"She probably will!" Jerusha said. "She's capable of it."

Olga's hands were trembling, and her hair was in disarray. She was dirty, and her experience had completely drained her of the ego that had always driven her. "If you had come in while she was here," she whispered, "she would have killed all three of you."

"I don't think she could have done that," Jerusha argued.

"Yes, she could. Something strange happened while she was in here. Her body—it started to glow. It started to glow green!"

"That's like the Denebians," Thrax murmured. He shifted his weight nervously and said once again, "We've got to get out of here."

Francesca Del Ray sipped her drink and smiled across at Sir Richard Irons. "You seem happy tonight, my dear," she said.

"I am happy. I'm thinking about how much fun I'm going to have with Zaria. That woman's given me nothing but trouble, and now it's my turn."

Francesca was wearing a metallic green dress. She was beautiful—as usual, he thought—but a troubled expression was on her face. "I'm not sure about that woman. I think we've got to be more careful."

"Careful? With her? She can't get out of that dungeon!"

"Somehow she was able to kill several men before being captured and brought aboard the *Jackray*. She's very powerful, Richard."

"She is at times." But Irons shrugged. "After she expends her powers, though, it apparently takes her a while to build back to full strength. Deneb and the green gaseous planets and her sources of help are a long way from here."

"Still, I advise getting rid of her right now," Del Ray murmured. "She feels herself to be a woman betrayed, and a woman in that condition—especially Zaria—is capable of anything."

"Are you speaking from experience, Francesca? I don't think—"

Irons did not finish his sentence. A hidden door known only to him—at least, so he had thought—suddenly burst open, and Mark Edge, Ringo Smith, and Ivan Petroski burst in, their Neuromags lifted.

"Stay right where you are, Irons!"

"Well, if it isn't my old friend, Captain Mark Edge. Glad to see you again, Captain."

"Which is a lie—like everything else that comes out of your mouth!"

"What are you doing here, Mark?" Francesca Del Ray gasped, rising to her feet and gaping at the intruder.

"The bad penny turns up again, eh, Francesca? I thought you might be tired of the situation here by this time, so I came back to give you a chance to get away —to rescue you, you might put it."

All three newcomers kept their Neuromags trained on Irons, but he sat totally at ease. He leaned back in his chair with a smile on his handsome face. "So. You've come to steal my second in command, have you? Anything else?"

"I may blow up your whole operation before I leave! I'm tired of your ways, Irons!"

"Why don't you start with me?" Irons said. "Go on. You've all got Neuromags. Go ahead and fire them. Wipe me out."

And before Edge could say anything, Ivan Petroski pulled the trigger.

Absolutely nothing happened.

"Maybe his Neuromag's out of order!" Irons mocked. "You other two—see what you can do!"

Instantly both Edge and Ringo Smith fired—or attempted to. But once again, nothing happened.

"You poor fools! Do you think I'd leave myself open to such threats as you might bring? Did you think I didn't know that you knew about my secret passageway? I've been waiting for you, Edge—ready for my revenge. I've had my quarters neutralized by the weapons defense system. Your weapons won't work here." His grin was evil. "But my weapons work fine." He lifted his voice then and said, "Fire, level one!"

At the sound of his voice command, three red rays shot from the ceiling module and struck Edge, Petroski, and Smith. Instantly the three were flung to the floor.

Getting to his feet, Sir Richard Irons casually walked over and smirked down at them. "Well, former pirate Edge, I bet that hurts a lot, doesn't it?"

Edge looked up and gasped, "You can't—"

"Fire, level two!" Irons called.

Three more red rays shot downward.

Edge managed to whisper, "I came—to bargain—for the lives—of the cadets you kidnapped."

"What do you think you possibly have to bargain with? You have nothing!"

"I've got one thing you want—the location of the tridium."

Irons's eyes narrowed. Tridium. That fabulously valuable metal that Mark Edge had located on a far-off planet while he was still in Sir Richard's service. He had escaped without revealing its location, and that had only further infuriated the pirate. "Oh, that's what you have, is it? Well, you'll tell me everything, anyway. I've only started working on you."

At that moment Ringo Smith tried to struggle to his feet. He fell to the floor again, but as he did, the medallion that he always wore around his neck dropped away from his armored suit.

Francesca Del Ray leaned over, gaping at the medallion. Then her hand went to her mouth, her eyes widened in shock, and she uttered a small cry.

"What's wrong with you, Francesca?" Irons shoved her aside and looked at what she saw. "You," he said then. "What's your name?"

Ringo could scarcely speak for the pain that racked his body. He tried to push the medallion back into the front of his body armor. "Ringo Smith," he said.

Irons reached down and jerked the medallion out of Ringo's hand. He gazed at it in silence for a moment, his face without expression. Then he said, "How is your father doing, Ringo Smith?"

Ivan Petroski was struggling to his knees. "Don't say anything to him, Ringo."

Irons turned and gave Petroski a vicious kick that slammed him against the wall, where he fell to the floor, hugging his side.

"Don't—say anything, Ringo!" Edge said. "Don't—give him—a thing!"

Irons pulled Ringo into a sitting position. He pushed his face down in front of the boy's and said, "Unless you talk, I will kill your two friends. Is that what you want?"

Ringo shook his head. He swallowed hard and said, "My father's dead."

Irons laughed, but it was not a pleasant sound. He examined Ringo's face closely, then turned to Francesca Del Ray and said, "It's the boy. It must be the boy."

"I knew it at once from the medallion."

"He looks a great deal like his mother," Irons remarked.

Ringo Smith gasped. "Did—did you know my mother?"

Bending over him, Irons said distinctly, "Of course, I knew your mother! She was my wife. And you, Ringo Smith, are my long lost son!"

Ringo could only stare up at Sir Richard Irons in total disbelief.

The pirate straightened up. "Where did you get that medallion?" he demanded.

"My—my mother gave it to me before she died."

"I'm sure she did. That medallion was your grandfather's. Wearing it makes you Lord Ringo Irons."

Ringo said, "I don't believe it! You're lying!"

"I think you know better than that. Look at the medallion—then look at me."

Ringo did not really need to look at the medallion, but he did. And he saw, as he glanced back at the man, that the image he had gazed at so often found reality in the classic features of Sir Richard Irons.

"So you have to believe that I'm your father, don't you? That medallion has been in our family for thousands of years, passed down from generation to generation." Then he snarled, and his face twisted. "To every generation except for me! Your grandfather denied me the medallion! He passed over me and gave it to *you*." Irons then glared at Francesca and said, "This is my son, all right!"

Ringo cried out, "Why did my mother leave home?"

Irons looked squarely at Ringo. "Because she knew I was going to kill you!"

Ringo Smith saw the hatred in his father's eyes, but he could not understand what he was hearing.

141

Irons continued, "My father—your grandfather—favored you over me. Over his son!"

"That's right," Francesca Del Ray murmured. "And so you killed your father and tried to kill your own son."

"I tried, but she escaped with him. I never saw her again."

Ringo staggered to his feet. "Well, she died. She died, thanks to you!"

Sir Richard smiled and said, "In a moment so will you—all of you—again thanks to me. And I will have the medallion." He lifted his head and said, "Fire, level—"

And then the wall of Irons's headquarters blew apart in a blaze of green light!

Bronwen and Contessa made their way up the maze of tunnels toward Irons's headquarters. It wasn't hard to follow the *Daystar* rescue party. She carried her electronically powered torch, and the markings on their shoe soles were easy to track.

The tunnel ended at a doorway that had been blasted away, presumably by Edge, Thrax, and the Rangers.

She assumed that the building was full of secret passageways. *Rats like Irons always have backup plans for a quick getaway*, she thought.

"All right, Contessa. My guess is that this is the way to Irons and this other passage is the way to the cell area." She started up the corridor that she assumed led to Sir Richard's headquarters.

Contessa bounded effortlessly behind her.

Then blaster shots sounded in the distance.

"We must hurry. There's not much time left!"

15

Zaria Finds Something New

As the wall exploded, Sir Richard Irons and Francesca Del Ray dashed to the other side of the office. Irons obviously could hardly believe what he was seeing with his own eyes. His headquarters was disintegrating in front of him, and his marvelous security system had done nothing to stop it.

Sir Richard faced the opposite wall and loudly yelled out a command. A voice lock was tripped. A panel slid back.

Even as Irons and Del Ray disappeared, Zaria entered, her eyes blazing and her body surrounded completely by an intense Denebian green glow.

The ceiling's defense module was shooting red rays all over the room. But the priestess aimed a finger at the module, and it exploded.

Still struggling to his feet, Captain Edge could only watch in wonderment. Somehow the woman had regained her unearthly powers.

Whirling quickly toward the *Daystar* crewmen, Zaria pointed again, and this time a thick green cloud drifted from her hand. It enveloped the three men, who immediately began coughing.

"I can't breathe!" Ringo choked.

"Zaria, don't do this thing!" Captain Edge gasped. It was as if he were breathing liquid fire.

"Let me hear you beg, Captain Edge!" The priestess laughed triumphantly. She stood straight, tall, and still beautiful. Her black hair flowed back over her shoulders, and her black eyes glowed with a greenish tint much like the glow that enveloped her. "Let me hear you beg! You would destroy me! Now it is I who will destroy you!"

"I can't make it, Captain!" Ivan Petroski's eyes rolled backward in his head, and he crumpled to the floor.

Edge, despite the pain that wracked his body, started toward Petroski. But then he stopped, knowing it was useless. He stood looking at the tall form of Zaria and waited.

"Zaria, don't kill them!" Ringo Smith was still upright but was leaning against a wall.

"You beg *me* for mercy! *Me*, Zaria, the Queen of Darkness?" Wild laughter issued from her lips.

And then the captain collapsed.

Through the same secret passageway the three men had used earlier, a small form entered.

Evidently Zaria sensed someone behind her. She whirled and found herself face to face with Bronwen Llewellen. "Not you!" she screamed. "Not you! I'll destroy you!"

Standing before the maniacal Zaria, Queen of Darkness, Bronwen Llewellen wore no body armor such as the other three wore. But she stood erect, and a smile came to her lips. She said in the gentlest of all tones, "No, Zaria, you will not destroy me. I represent One whose powers are far greater than yours."

And then, holding herself even straighter, Bronwen extended her arm directly toward the high priestess. She called out in a powerful voice, more powerful than anyone would have expected from a small woman, "Lord Jesus, command these wicked spirits to depart!"

Instantly, the swirling green light began to fade—
it was as if it had been turned down by a powered
switch—until finally all the luminous green was gone,
and Zaria dropped to the floor, her face white as chalk.

Mark Edge had no choice but to regain consciousness. Contessa was licking his face, and this time the captain was glad to see her. He lurched to his feet, wondering briefly what Bronwen was doing here and what had
happened to Zaria. But all seemed to be under control.

Ringo was sitting up. Ivan lay motionless. The captain knew that he and Ringo—still recovering from
Zaria's green gas—could not carry the crew chief. With
his belt, Edge tied Ivan onto the big dog's back and sent
her trotting off into the tunnel.

"Let's get back to the *Daystar*, Bronwen," he said.
Then Edge helped Ringo to his feet, and they staggered
toward the hidden corridor.

While never taking her eyes off Zaria, Bronwen
saw her young friends disappear into the secret corridor. Then she murmured, "Thank You, Lord Jesus," and
knelt beside the fallen sorceress.

Pulling Zaria up to a sitting position, Bronwen put
an arm around the priestess and gently held her. When
the woman opened her eyes, Bronwen whispered with
as much love as she could muster, "Daughter, you are
only moments away from eternity."

Perhaps Zaria, Queen of Darkness, for the first
time in her life knew fear. She certainly well knew
what awaited her on the other side of this life. She had
seen enough of dark and evil things. She began to cry.

Bronwen held the woman tenderly, as a mother
would hold her daughter, trying to remember that this
was just a human being who had gone far into evil.

145

Looking upward, she breathed a prayer, saying, "Lord Jesus, You died for sinners. This, my Lord, is a sinner that You died for." She looked then at the priestess. "But, Zaria, I think for the first time since you were a child, you are free from the control of Satan and his dark angels. Is that not so, my daughter?"

Zaria reached out a hand pitifully.

It was grasped by Bronwen Llewellen, who said, "Is it true that you are now free from the powers that have held you for so long?"

Zaria managed to speak. "Yes, they're gone. I had forgotten what it was like to be free from them."

"Zaria, the Lord Jesus loves you and desires for you to live with Him for eternity. He died on a cross for you, for me, for all people. Can you believe this, Zaria?"

Zaria's eyes suddenly filled with tears, and Bronwen wiped them away.

"Zaria, those who call on the name of the Lord will be saved. Can you do that?"

"Yes, I can." Zaria's face, which had been twisted with hatred so long, suddenly changed. "I've wasted my life, Lord," she cried, "but—if this woman tells the truth—Jesus died for me. I believe that. Please, Lord, save me in the name of Your Son, Jesus."

Zaria was speaking in a hoarse whisper that could barely be heard. She continued to pray, telling God that she was sorry for her sins and asking Jesus to come into her life. "Please," she whispered, "be my Savior even as You are the Savior of this woman."

The hard light faded from Zaria's eyes, and it was replaced by an expression of joy and peace. Bronwen could almost see heaven in her face.

"It's true," Zaria whispered, slipping by seconds out into eternity. "It's always been true what you said, Bronwen Llewellen. Jesus is Lord of all."

"And is He your Lord now, Zaria?"

"Yes, He has come to me. I am His. I . . . thank you . . . for loving me . . ."

And then she was gone.

With tears on her own cheeks, Bronwen Llewellen gently laid back Zaria's body. She gave one look at the peaceful expression on the still face and whispered, "Thank You, God, for Your mercy."

Suddenly the room began to shake as if from an earthquake. Bronwen threw herself at the doorway, calling out, "Lord, help me make it back to the ship!"

Dai dropped off Karl Bentlow at sick bay. Standing by the bed, Dai looked down at the boy he had just rescued. "Karl, if you can hear me—" Dai took his hand "—Dr. Cole will be here in a minute. She'll fix you up, although it looks to me that you will be very sore for a while." Dai rubbed his own shoulder. "I know I would hate to be shot in the shoulder."

Dai felt Karl's hand squeeze his.

"I have to go. My aunt's not back yet, and I need to see if she needs help."

As Dai left sick bay, Dr. Cole came in, went to Karl's bed, and began treating him.

Jerusha stood waiting with Raina by the tunnel entrance. "I can hear someone coming," she said, "but it sounds very . . . odd."

Suddenly she heard an angry yell. Then there was laughing. Jerusha didn't know who was screaming, but she recognized the captain's laugh easily.

Raina was very puzzled. "What is he laughing about? We've got to get out of here, and he's laughing?"

Contessa ran at full gallop out from the secret tunnel with Ivan Petroski tied to her back.

The chief engineer's arms flailed the air. He was shouting curses at apparently anyone he could think of —especially Contessa. "You mangy daughter of a flea-bitten swamp dog. When I get this belt off me, I'm going to beat you into a whimpering pile of canine by-products."

Captain Edge and Ringo followed Contessa from the tunnel. The captain was still laughing, but as much from relief as from amusement. It was obvious that his good friend Ivan Petroski was on his way to full recovery from his recent ordeal.

"Hold on there, Ivan. I'll get you loose." Edge worked at the belt. It had become twisted so that it was hard to loosen.

Ivan's face was red with rage. "I promise you, Mark Edge, as soon as you untie me, I'm going to knock you into next year."

"Will you, really?" Edge asked, still struggling to control his laughter.

"Just let me go—you'll rue the day, I tell you!"

Edge knelt by the dog. "Take him to Studs, Contessa. Find Studs. Studs. He can fight with him."

The huge German shepherd loped off obediently toward the *Daystar*. The chief engineer shouted threats with every step.

Just then Edge saw Dai Bando, alarm on his face, run down the gangplank and race toward him. "Where's my Aunt Bronwen?"

Edge swung around toward the tunnel entrance, suddenly realizing that his navigator had not followed them. "I don't know, Dai. But she's all right. Believe me, your aunt's God has more power than all the weapons on *Daystar* combined."

And then he heard—was it *singing?* Faint at first, the melody grew louder and louder, and then Bronwen appeared at the mouth of the tunnel. Her face was beaming, but tears streamed down her cheeks. She was singing some song of praise to God.

Edge and Dai Bando looked at each other in bewilderment.

She ran right by them, then shouted back, "We've got to get off this moon. I think it's going to blow!"

Edge called everyone back to the *Daystar* and made sure everyone was manning his station. The ship lifted and thrust over to the watery tunnel, where it dropped out of sight.

16
The Celebration

Many light-years away from the *Daystar*, a lone ship—it was the *Jackray*—raced away from the Pegasus Sector at top speed. Sir Richard Irons stood on the bridge, monitoring the main view screen.

Francesca Del Ray joined him and linked her arm in his. Despite their harrowing escape from Zaria, she looked as beautiful as ever. Her blonde hair cascaded across her shoulders. Her blue silk dress accented her blue eyes perfectly.

Irons knew Francesca very well. She wanted to know something.

"Richard, sometimes your anger scares even me." She rested her head on his shoulder. "I've never understood what you have to fear from that one small boy."

Irons turned and pulled up Francesca's chin until her face was close to his. "As long as that boy is alive," he explained grimly, "the family bloodline will make every effort to give him *my* kingdom."

"How can that be?"

"It's that medallion he wears. The first lord of the Irons family crafted it in the bowels of the planet Merlina. That planet has always had a magical quality. That's why Zaria has always been so attracted to it. When the first lord formed the medallion, it appears that some superhuman power affixed itself to it. Every lord of the Irons family for thousands of years has worn it. And now *he* has it—the boy—with all its powers."

Sir Richard turned away from Francesca and, eyes

narrowed, stared out into the darkness. "Someday, though, there will come a reckoning between young Ringo and myself. And it will be *me* who picks the time and the place."

As the *Daystar* plunged through the vastness of space and the glittering stars flashed by like long lines of light, the cruiser's chow hall was filled with the sound of laughter and excitement. Raina had organized a party for Ringo, and everyone was there except for Karl Bentlow, who was still in sick bay.

When Ringo entered, he could hardly believe his eyes. The Space Rangers had made special decorations out of their clothes and whatever else they could find on *Daystar*. Jerusha had raided Heck's clothes closet and tied together fifty of his most outlandish-looking scarves. Then she'd hung them from the ceiling like streamers.

Actually, Ringo thought, *they look better than streamers.*

Heck Jordan's scarves were a variety of colors— and that was ironic, because Heck himself could not distinguish one color from another. He believed that all the scarves looked the same. Heck had so many of them because he hated washing his clothes.

The grunts had participated by stringing sparkling colored lights around the hall in different patterns, and Bronwen Llewellen made several gallons of her special punch. Throughout the evening, crew members had made a point of coming up to Ringo and saying nice things.

In spite of all the attention, however, Ringo stood in the middle of the room and felt like an outsider more than ever.

Dai Bando and his Aunt Bronwen lounged by one of the refreshment tables, sipping punch and eating cake.

"I still can hardly believe your story about Zaria, Aunt," he said. "For such a long time we'd heard horrible things about her, and now to think that she suddenly is in heaven. She didn't have much time as a Christian, did she?"

"No, but if she had lived, I think she would have been a good one. God chose to take her home."

Dai gave his favorite aunt a smile and put an arm around her. "And if you hadn't listened to His prompting and gone to Sir Richard's headquarters, I don't think any of us would have made it out alive. She would have killed us all—she or Sir Richard."

"I'm getting a little bit old for such adventures. Someday soon, you're going to have to take over for me, Dai."

"Me? I could never take your place."

"The Lord has a special work for you to do. He has assured me of that. Now—why don't you go talk to Mei-Lani? She looks lonesome over there all alone."

Captain Edge and Dr. Cole made a handsome couple. He was in dress uniform, and the gown that she had chosen to wear was made of rose-colored silk. She wore a necklace of sparkling green stones that caught the light as she moved.

"Mark, I was so happy—so relieved—when I saw you coming back from Irons's headquarters. I had the most awful feeling the whole time you were gone."

"You mean you were worried about me or about all of us?"

"I meant *they*, but there was some *he* in it, too. You're the *he*."

She remembered the terrible tension. For a time, she'd found herself gripped by an anxiety that she had never known before.

The captain smiled wryly and said, "One of these days I'm going to become the kind of man who is worth worrying about."

Temple Cole looked up at him, thinking, *He doesn't know how good-looking he is—and that's a good thing. He doesn't know how I feel about him, either—and that's probably a good thing, too.*

She said in a teasing way, "I have a list that I'll give you of all the things I would like to see in a man."

"Give them to me, Doc. I'll start in on them at once!"

The sick bay door opened, and Karl Bentlow looked up to see Jerusha entering. She carried a tray with a slice of cake and a large glass of punch on it.

"I didn't want you to get left out, Karl," she said. She set down the tray and handed him the cake plate. Then she sat down beside his bed. "How are you feeling?"

"Like I've been dragged through a knothole," he admitted. He knew he had lost weight through his ordeal. People had told him even his face was thin.

"You had a hard time. For a while there it was nip and tuck whether Dr. Temple would be able to pull you out of it or not."

He chewed a bite of cake. "I can't remember much about that. It's all kind of like a bad dream."

Glancing around the room, Jerusha asked, "Where's Olga? This is the first time I've been here when she was gone."

Karl grinned. "Heck showed up a few minutes ago. He took her up with him to look over the bridge."

Jerusha chuckled. "Olga has no idea what she's in for."

"What does that mean?"

"Oh, nothing. Except that Heck thinks he's quite a Romeo."

"It might not be bad if some guy *would* take an interest in Olga," Karl said. "I know you don't like her. Not many people do."

"Well, she gave us a hard time back at the Academy, Karl."

"Yes, she did. But then, so did I. I've never asked you to forgive me for that, Jerusha—but I do now. I'm sorry."

She said quickly, "Apology accepted. I did hold hard feelings once, but no more. Here, drink your punch."

"And I haven't ever really thanked you for saving my life, either—mine and Olga's both."

"Why, it was a team effort, Karl."

"I know that, but when you were beside me on that cell floor, somehow your touch was special." Suddenly he set down the punch glass on the bedside table and took hold of Jerusha's arm. Then he drew her down and kissed her soundly on the cheek.

"Why, Karl Bentlow, I'm surprised at you! You shouldn't—"

At that moment Zeno Thrax walked in. He stopped and stared at them with his pale albino eyes. "Am I interrupting anything?" he asked with a small smile.

Jerusha pulled herself free. Her face was red. "Of course not!" she snapped. She hurried past him and out the door.

Karl had a big smile on his face.

Looking down at him, Zeno said innocently, "Well, Bentlow, you're looking much better now than you did before you looked like this."

Karl Bentlow gave a joyous laugh. He put out his

hand to shake Zeno's and said, "I feel a whole lot more like I do now than I did before I felt like this."

The two men fell silent for a few seconds, perhaps trying to figure out what they had just said.

Though the bridge of the *Daystar* was a familiar place to Heck Jordan, Olga found it new and fascinating. She had been surprised when Heck appeared with his invitation but had willingly enough agreed to accompany him to the bridge.

Now the Space Ranger was talking about the new long-range sensors that he had invented, and she listened with interest. Actually, she wasn't as interested in Heck as she was in the sensors.

"Show me how they work, Heck."

"Sure!" He brought her to the scanning console and switched the sensors to their longest setting.

She watched as he performed, and she was much impressed. "I think you've done a wonderful job. It's quite ingenious, really!"

Heck seemed to want to compliment Olga in return but couldn't think of anything to say. What he came up with was, "Well, I certainly admire your taste in men." Then, apparently realizing that was not exactly right, he said hurriedly, "Wait just a minute. Let me tend to this."

Heck was about to switch the scanners back to normal range when he looked closely at the screen and said, "I wonder what that is."

Olga looked over the data that came from the scanner, then remarked, "Well, this beats anything I ever saw!"

He adjusted a couple of switches that fine-tuned the detail on the viewer. "They look like *insect* pods more than anything else I can think of. I've never heard of Magnum-Deep-Space-Cruiser-sized insect pods, though."

The objects that Olga and Heck scanned were indeed the size of large cruisers. Dark brown-and-green mottling spangled the sides of each pod. The ends of the pods were crimped closed. The scanners indicated that there were more than one hundred fifty of them in this group. Other clusters of pods were much farther away.

Heck stared at the screen, mystified. "They really aren't ships. They're nonmetallic."

The two young people studied the view screen for a few minutes until, finally, Olga murmured, "One of them is *larger* than a Magnum Deep Space Cruiser."

"And see? They don't have any propulsion systems, either. They look like they're adrift," he said. "Oh, well, they're light-years away from the Pegasus system. If we ever meet up with them, it won't be anytime soon. That's for sure."

Olga said, "Do you think maybe we ought to go report it, anyway?"

"Nah. Believe me. They're too distant to worry about. Want to go down to Ringo's party with me, Olga?"

Olga looked up at Heck, and a pleased look came over her plain face. "You know, Heck, it's been a long time since someone asked me to a party."

"Well, you picked a winner this time, Olga. I'm the best partyer on the whole ship—or anywhere else for that matter. Come on. Let's go see what's going on."

Ever since they had escaped from Richard Irons's stronghold, Ringo had been stunned by what he had learned about himself. It had been bad enough to have *no* parents, but now to learn that Sir Richard Irons—

perhaps the most villainous man in the cosmos—was his father . . . Ringo had kept to himself and stayed unusually quiet, even for him.

This party had caught him off guard. He kept looking around the room and feeling awkward and out of place. And then he heard a teasing voice say, "Ringo, could I have the first dance?" He spun around.

It was Raina St. Clair. She had put on a dress he had never seen before. It was pale green with tiny diamond-like flakes in it, and her auburn hair was crowned with a silver tiara. Her eyes were bright, and there was a wide smile on her lips as she stood waiting for him to respond.

"I couldn't dance even if anybody wanted to, Raina. Dancing is just one more thing I'm not smart enough to do."

"Don't *say* things like that, Ringo Smith!"

Astonished, he gaped at her outburst.

"I keep telling you—you can do most anything you really want to. What people enjoy doing is what they can do well, and God has made you able to do a lot of things well. You've always been one to put yourself down, Ringo, and I want this day to be the day when you stop doing that."

"I don't know if I can."

"What's *really* wrong, Ringo? You ought to be happy. This party is in your honor. Everything aboard *Daystar* has gone so well—we've carried out our mission. And now you've finally found out about your father . . ."

Ringo was silent for a few seconds. Then he sighed. "And I wish I hadn't," he said. "Imagine having *Sir Richard Irons* as your father. The worst pirate in the whole galaxy!"

"You have to look at the positive side of things,

Ringo. Your father is *alive*. And while he's alive, there's still hope for him!"

Raina was looking at Ringo so closely that he turned his eyes away from her.

"Is *that* why you've been so quiet lately?" she asked.

"I can't stand the thought of it, Raina. He— Richard Irons is nothing but a murderer. He would have killed my mother and me both, if she hadn't managed to get away with me."

"You've forgotten something."

"Forgotten what?" he demanded. He felt tears in his eyes and hated himself for it. "I'm nothing but the son of a murderer. I haven't forgotten *that.*"

"Have you forgotten Zaria?"

Of course, Ringo had heard that story. They all had. Bronwen Llewellen had told of how Zaria had turned to God and had been forgiven just before her death.

"What about her?" he asked.

"She was an evil woman—far more given over to evil than even Sir Richard Irons—but God found her, and she's now safe in heaven. Made clean and forgiven. God can do that even for the people we think are hopeless."

Ringo was struck by what Raina said, but he did not answer for a time. Then he looked directly at her and asked, "You mean, then, that you truly think there's hope for my father?"

"There's hope for everyone, Ringo. It's up to you to pray for him. And for all your friends—like me, and Mei-Lani, and Jerusha—to pray, too. Why, we'll all join with you in doing that."

"And you really think a man like that can find the Lord . . ."

"You've read the Bible. You know he can. Let's watch and see what God does. Now, come on. We're going to have a good time at this party." She reached up suddenly and touched his cheek. "I'm so glad that you're all right. I–I worried about you, Ringo."

He smiled and made up his mind. Whatever might happen in the future, Ringo Smith at that moment would be happy.

Moody Press, a ministry of the Moody Bible Institute, is designed for education, evangelization, and edification. If we may assist you in knowing more about Christ and the Christian life, please write us without obligation: Moody Press, c/o MLM, Chicago, Illinois 60610.